Hᴏᴡ ᴀᴘᴛ ᴛʜᴀᴛ [...] asked me to writ[e...] their own tenth anniversary. My first book for LOVE-SWEPT, *Surrender*, was published in their launch month, May 1983, as book #2. And we've both gone full steam ahead since then!

Surrender was about a strong woman, feisty, full of character and courage, the sort of heroine I enjoy writing about. And over the last ten years, I've continued to tell love stories of strong-willed women and the forceful men they fall in love with. Taking this occasion of LOVESWEPT's tenth anniversary to look back, I'm proud of what we've accomplished, the freedom and latitude my editors have allowed me in writing romances that stretch traditional boundaries, and our mutual, continual success.

My book this month, *'Til We Meet Again*, revolves around an anniversary, a tenth high school reunion. Once again, an indomitable force—the hero, Cole Whitford—meets an immovable object—his lover from ten years earlier, Del Peters. Throughout the book, they struggle to find the love they lost ten years earlier, and to fit together their much changed lives.

That, to me, is what anniversaries are all about—people, what they are, what they do. Just as I have an undying interest in people, I shall always love and celebrate—and try to learn from—anniversaries.

Helen Mittermeyer

WHAT ARE *LOVESWEPT* ROMANCES?

They are stories of true romance and touching emotion. We believe those two very important ingredients are constants in our highly sensual and very believable stories in the LOVESWEPT *line. Our goal is to give you, the reader, stories of consistently high quality that may sometimes make you laugh, sometimes make you cry, but are always fresh and creative and contain many delightful surprises within their pages.*

Most romance fans read an enormous number of books. Those they truly love, they keep. Others may be traded with friends and soon forgotten. We hope that each LOVESWEPT *romance will be a treasure—a "keeper." We will always try to publish*

LOVE STORIES YOU'LL NEVER FORGET
BY AUTHORS YOU'LL ALWAYS REMEMBER

The Editors

**'TIL WE
MEET AGAIN**

HELEN
MITTERMEYER

BANTAM BOOKS
NEW YORK · TORONTO · LONDON · SYDNEY · AUCKLAND

'TIL WE MEET AGAIN

A Bantam Book / June 1993

If you would be interested in receiving protective vinyl
covers for your Loveswept books, please write to this
address for information:

Loveswept
Bantam Books
P.O. Box 985
Hicksville, NY 11802

ISBN 0-553-44243-0

Published simultaneously in the United States and Canada

PRINTED IN THE UNITED STATES OF AMERICA

OPM   0 9 8 7 6 5 4 3 2 1

PROLOGUE

She was in love with Coletrane Whitford, and he loved her. He'd told her so, over and over again when they made love in the backseat of his father's Chevrolet. For the first time in her life Fidelia Peters Madison felt wanted, cherished, important.

Her parents didn't see it that way. After all, Cole was five years older than she, and had been to college, the local branch of the State University of New York in Geneseo. And they considered him "fast."

"You're only eighteen, Fidelia," her mother would say. At fifty-four years old, Del's mother was even more conservative than she'd been as a prim, stay-at-home young lady who'd married the only person she'd ever dated, Peter Madison. Alice and Peter had lived in Geneseo all their lives, except for a year when Peter had taken a job downstate with another telephone company. Alice had been so homesick for her hometown, her husband had gotten his old job back and they'd returned, married one year, with an infant girl.

Whenever the subject of Fidelia's dating Cole came up, Peter just sighed. He'd worked for over thirty years at the switching center for the phone company and wanted to leave Geneseo and go to Florida, where it was warm, where he could golf, and be near the cronies whom he'd worked with for over thirty years. "I'm retiring soon," he'd announce for the hundredth time, as though he were telegraphing some awesome news.

Fidelia felt as though a plastic shield separated her from her parents. She was sure they'd have given anything to call back that intemperate moment when she was conceived. It wasn't that she was abused; she just felt in the way, a third wheel, an unpleasant after-thought. She wanted to love them. She just couldn't reach them. She had an uneasy certainty that they felt the same way.

Cole was different. He was dynamic, warm, and so very reachable. He held her and kissed her. Her folks had never done that in all her life. They were conservative, restrained, and were appalled that their daughter wasn't. "She's a throwback to your mother, Alice," Peter would say.

"She deserted the family, ran off with a banjo play-er," Alice would add darkly. "My father bore the burden of that, and my sister Lena and I had to raise ourselves almost. Lena had a touch of that same wildness." Her pinched lips revealed her disapproval. "Fidelia, you're like your Aunt Lena."

"I liked Aunt Lena," Fidelia would say. "I was sorry when she died."

"Bound to come to a bad end," her mother would mutter.

Del was positive her parents came from a Victorian time warp. They were just as sure their daughter was the result of bad genes that had lain dormant in most of the family and were now rearing their ugly head once again.

From almost the moment Del became close to Cole she began telling him everything—how she was doing in school, her hopes and dreams for the future, how she loved math when most of her friends despised it, how she'd even tried doing her father's income tax for him. Her father had just frowned and said it wasn't the kind of thing she should be doing. "Learn to bake a cherry pie like your mother, Fidelia. And start making your own clothes. You'll save money. That's what proper girls do."

Fidelia hated sewing. Baking was a messy bore. She'd rather draw illustrations for the children's story she'd written, or do math. She didn't try to explain that to her father.

She told Cole about the illustrations, about the story, how she had fun doing math.

He laughed. "I like math and science, too, Del, so I understand. But I guess I'm going to be a lawyer instead of a farmer like my mother's father. My father and grandfather want me to become a partner in their firm."

"Well, lawyers need to know about math and science."

He kissed her then, and she forgot about everything as she clung to him with the mindless gratitude of the unloved for the loving. Cole was all the warmth she'd been seeking all her life. She couldn't spend enough time with him.

And he had a car. Most of her friends had trucks. His father owned a horse farm several miles outside of town, but he'd gone to the local high school and then on to the small SUNY school in Geneseo. They met when he was in the master's program, doing an elective in tutoring. He'd become a teacher's aide at the high school as part of his interning program. Such out-of-class studies looked good on the applications he'd sent to various law schools, he told Del when he helped her on an advanced history course.

They didn't date, just spoke when they saw each other. The next year, though, when he was in his second year of the master's program and she was a freshman at the university, he finally asked her out.

After that they became inseparable.

Around Christmastime, Cole discovered he'd been accepted as a Fulbright scholar. He was going to Japan for a year, then he'd enter Cornell Law School.

"I'm happy for you," Del sobbed on his shoulder.

"Aw, honey, I hate to leave you. But I'll be back. I promise."

They were in his dad's car, parked on a high hill looking toward the Southern Tier of New York. "I'd hoped for this Fulbright, Del. I wanted it badly. Now, I want to chuck it."

"You'll be gone a whole year," she said desperately. "Hold me."

They kissed, the passion flaming between them, the fire all but consuming them.

"Honey, don't! I won't be able to stop—"

"Then don't. I belong to you. I want you to love me."

"Oh, Del, baby, I love you. But I want to protect you, honey. Wait—"

"I don't want to wait. I love you." She wouldn't see him for a whole year! "I wish you didn't have to go."

"So do I, now."

"Love me, Cole."

"Oh, baby, I want you."

"And I want you." If she'd had her choice they'd have been in a big wide bed with satin sheets, not in the back of his father's car. Someday.

When she felt his hands on her bare skin, she shivered with joy. Then they were skin to skin and trembling. Their desire burned through all the good reasons why they should hold back, why safe sex was so important, why they should wait. Despair at their imminent parting, longing, and a great desire to give to each other mixed in them, firing their passion to white heat. Del clung to Cole, happy to be joined to him.

"Oh, I love you, Cole."

"And I love you, Del . . . forever."

ONE

Reunion! She was really there. Her ten-year high school reunion.

Where had the years gone? She might've remained in Geneseo, if she hadn't gotten pregnant in her first year in college. Instead of continuing her education, she'd gone to Florida with her parents, given birth, and started a new life.

"Stop sighing. We'll have a good time," her friend Marge said at her back, urging her into the cavernous gymnasium, decorated like a French restaurant, where the dance would be held.

"I can hardly wait," Del muttered, trying to smile. "Why are they having it here and not at a restaurant?"

Marge shrugged. "Foul-up, from what I hear. Our chairman didn't confirm, and we lost out." She looked around. "This isn't bad." She winced as the band tuned up. "Of course, the noise level will be high because it's a basketball court, but at least there'll be plenty of room. Oh, look, they have sidewalk tables with umbrellas around the bar. Very Place Pigalle."

Del laughed, noticing the trellises festooned with flowers, the small round tables decorated with the school colors. As people congregated and milled about, the noise level did increase, but somehow it seemed friendly. Del pointed up at the ceiling, which was coated with multicolored balloons. "Maybe it will be fun."

"Good." Marge looked around, her eyes alight. "Oh, oh, there's Dina. I'd better go. I said I'd help. Mingle, mingle."

Del watched her friend disappear in the crowd and exhaled resignedly. She wished she was back at Marge's with her daughter, Laurie, and Marge's two children, eating the barbecue the sitter would be fixing for them.

She should have waited for her fiftieth reunion. Her memories of her last year in Geneseo were still too fresh. She could almost see Cole. He'd stand out, though there were a number of tall men; his six-foot-three, well-muscled frame always did. Why wasn't her memory of him hazy, and blurred, instead of sharp, three-dimensional clear? Bigger than life: That was Cole. In twenty lifetimes he wouldn't fade from her mind, and she'd sure tried her damnedest to eradicate him. As though she'd conjured him up, she envisioned him right in front of her. Sleek muscles had given him the strength and quickness needed for basketball and swimming, and he'd lettered in both. The twist in his classic nose, the dimples at the side of his mouth gave him a rakish visage, and added to his masculinity. She remembered his square jaw, his endearing, persuasive smile, the one eyetooth that had been expensively rebuilt after being broken during rough play on the court. Those long fingers flexing on her skin, how his biceps had felt under her hands when he held her while dancing. How she'd loved to run her fingers through his thick ebony hair. His eyes had mesmerized her, deep hazel and flecked with gold. Too damned handsome for his own good. But he'd been gentle with her, and she'd been overwhelmed that he'd chosen her.

Del squeezed her eyes shut, her body boiling and freezing with memory. It was humiliating to recall how much she'd wanted him, shocking to realize he could still make her feel so hot. She shouldn't have come to this reunion, she should've waited fifty years. No, a hundred. It was all she could do not to gallop to the exit, grab any car that had keys in it, find Laurie, and hightail it back to Florida.

Only loyalty to Marge kept her where she was.

When the music began it was a relief to concentrate on something besides Cole. She moved back into the shadows of the flickering multihued Chinese lanterns and let the music take her away, away from Geneseo and Cole.

It was Del!

At first Cole had thought it was the confusion of

the crowd, the noise, the many handshakes, laughter, colored lights, balloons. But it wasn't. She was there at the joint class reunion, watching the dancing couples. It couldn't be Del. But it was.

Smells came from beyond the gym where the catering staff had set up a makeshift kitchen. At any other time he would've tried to identify the myriad aromas, but now he didn't even notice. All of his senses were focused on Del. He brushed absently at some colored streamers that touched his face, his gaze never leaving her.

He would have known her anywhere. She was still taller than most of the women standing near her, but she was even more slender than he remembered. Her long body and longer legs looked almost fragile, though ten years ago they had couched some very silky muscles and sinew that had driven him wild with wanting.

Her hands had aroused him as much as her perfect breasts. They were supple and expressive, those hands, with long fingers. She'd used them when she talked, running them through her hair, lifting them high, spreading them to make a point, throwing them wide when she laughed. Her long, indented waist and smoothly curving hips hadn't changed. He couldn't see the color of her eyes in the whirling strobes of light that cast multihued shadows on the walls. Were they still sea green, round, gemlike?

And was her hair still red gold? He couldn't tell in the dimness, but it shone each time a light of any color touched it. She wore it shorter now, more businesslike, but there was still a cluster of curls on top that swirled down toward her forehead. Her beautiful cheekbones were more pronounced. She had the angelic beauty she'd had before, but there was a sophistication to it, a wall around her that was new.

Was her skin still like velvet porcelain? Once he couldn't get enough of kissing it, her arms, neck, face, breasts . . . lower.

Desire cascaded through him, spinning him as if he were a raft in the floodwaters of the Genesee. It was followed swiftly by bitterness, though. How could he still want her when she'd turned her back on him, left the area, stopped writing, even when he'd sent her letter after letter? She'd wanted nothing to do with him.

Dueling desires—to ignore her or to speak to her—jousted inside him. He took a deep breath and melted back into the shadows, watching, watching.

If Marge's husband hadn't been out of town, Del thought, if Marge hadn't wheedled, if the children didn't have such a good sitter . . . She ran all the ifs through her mind, edging as she did toward the exit. She might be able to get a ride home with someone leaving early. She'd explain to Marge first, of course. They'd been friends since grade school, and Del didn't have a closer confidante. Only Marge could've persuaded her to come back from Florida . . . and she was beginning to regret she'd done so.

"Del! Del Madison, how are you?"

She turned. "Why Jim . . . Daryl . . . Bonnie. It's good to see you."

Within minutes Del's trepidation melted away in the burst of talk from old friends. She joined them in the old stories, laughing, relaxing, glad suddenly that she was there. Not all the memories were bad, she was beginning to realize.

Surprisingly, the reunion continued to be fun. Several more former classmates gathered around and began reminiscing. It was friendly, open, enjoyable, as tales flew back and forth.

Del was laughing after listening to one anecdote involving her and Marge, when she felt a light tap on her shoulder. Still mirthful, she turned . . . and almost fainted.

"Dance?"

She could only stare stupidly. "Cole?"

"Yes. How are you, Del?"

"I didn't know you lived in this area." She'd never have come back if she had. "You're a lawyer . . . in California." She could've bitten through her tongue when he looked pleased, as though he felt she'd kept tabs on him. "I didn't check," she added. "Someone told me. You're married, have a family." Why didn't she shut up? He was still gorgeous. He could still turn her to jelly. Where was his wife?

"I don't mind if you check up on me."

She caught his scowl. "I didn't!" Red-faced when heads turned at her loud tone, she lowered her voice. "I didn't check on you," she muttered, looking around for Marge.

"Looking for someone?"

"Marge," she mumbled, her gaze roving the crowd.

"Marge is dancing," he said. "And I asked you. Remember?"

"Of course I remember. I'm not senile," she snapped, keeping her trembling hands behind her. He was bigger than she'd remembered, and he looked wonderful in a casual evening suit, the summer silk clinging to his body as though it had been sewn on him. He didn't just dress well, he was smashingly understated. And he was making her sweat. Not glow, or even perspire, but sweat. She'd soon soak her clothes. "I have to go."

"No, you don't," he said easily.

She looked around, seeing that all of her old friends had melted away. "Excuse me." She had to get away, she had to think.

"No. Let's dance, Del. Or would you like to go a couple of rounds?" Her hesitation had him laughing, and she held up her arms stiffly, glowering at him. She was tempted to land a haymaker right in the middle of his grin. Her fists curled with an almost irrepressible desire. When his strong arms closed around her, she was sure her body had liquefied, that she was going to dribble to the floor into a puddle. Her knees were soft gelatin. A tingling awareness went through her bones to her soul. She felt giddy, girlish . . . stupid. Self-control, idiot, she told herself. Self-control. She was stronger than this. She would stand firm. No, she couldn't, she was dancing. It was heaven . . . hell. "Actually, I don't dance much anymore."

He laughed, tightening his arm around her. "I haven't seen you for ten years and that's the first thing you tell me? You couldn't have changed so radically. We danced constantly. Remember? I do. You couldn't get enough of it."

"My feet aren't what they used to be," she improvised.

He glanced down. "Bunions?"

"No," she said indignantly.

"Ah, corns. Soak 'em every night?"

"No! And I'm not creaking in my rocking chair, either."

"Good. Then we can dance."

"Your wife here?" Another leading question! Damn her runaway mouth. She winced when he smiled. Besides, she didn't want to hear the answer to that question, nor did she want to meet his spouse.

He pulled her closer, their bodies touching from knee to collarbone, and put his mouth to her hair. "I never married, Del. Almost did a couple of times, but I had so many years of . . . Well, let's just say I didn't marry. Are you still Del Madison?"

"No . . . no. I'm Del Peters, now. I live in Florida.

I've been there quite a while. . . ." *And I cried for you, damn your hide, Whitford.*

"Married down there?"

"I'm . . . not married. I do have a family, though."

He nodded. "Single-parent families are not uncommon." His smile twisted. "And a great many of our friends are divorced. But you have children, and that should help. I always wanted a family."

"*Child.* Just one. A girl." Her mouth had turned into a rivet gun, but she couldn't bring herself to go into an in-depth explanation. It was all too macabre, having him there, Laurie's father. The man whom her parents had castigated to her as a user, a manipulator, an immoral person, over and over again, the man who'd joined her in sinning, as her parents saw it. They had tried to forgive her, and she'd tried to be a dutiful daughter for the short time they'd lived after Laurie's birth. It saddened her that she'd hurt her parents so much, but she'd never regretted Laurie's birth. Only Marge and her husband Sid knew her story. Laurie knew that her father was a lawyer in California. But that wasn't true anymore. When they were back in Florida Del would talk to her. Cole was here! In front of her! Dancing with her. Great heavens.

She didn't know how to deal with the reality of being with him again. It was a cruel travesty of the dreams she'd had at the very beginning of her pregnancy. Cole would come. He'd take care of her. She'd be safe. He'd hold her in his arms as he always did, and nothing would hurt her, no one could harm her. He was her bastion and she didn't have to fear. Cruel and stupid and foolish.

Cole swung her out from his body in an old remembered gesture, and her body responded at once. She closed her eyes for a moment as though she could hold the touch of ecstasy longer, as though she could capture and keep the moment in time.

"I missed you," Cole said when he brought her back to him.

Del trembled and opened her eyes. She said nothing, her throat so full, so choked with yesterday and her memories, she couldn't speak.

"Are you going to stay in Florida?" he asked.

She nodded. Of course she was going back to Florida, preferably deep into the Everglades where he'd never find her or Laurie. What would he say about his daughter, about having a daughter? She closed her mind to the spectrum of possibilities.

"Do you like it?"

She nodded again. Were there deep caves in Florida? Did one have to swim to reach them? No matter, she'd find a safe hole for her and Laurie.

He leaned back a fraction. "Aren't you ever going to talk to me again?"

She swallowed and coughed. "Are—are you a lawyer in this area?" Her voice was hoarse, the words forced from her throat. He'd probably know just how to sue her so that she'd be in jail for a hundred years. But that was ridiculous. He had no reason to be angry with her. He'd gone off to Japan with his Fulbright in hand. She'd stayed behind and had a child alone. She sensed a menace in him, but by heaven if he tried to act against her, she'd tear a strip off him. No—what she had to do was get back to Florida and her life. Laurie needed her.

Laurie needed a father too, an unwelcome voice said deep inside her.

Cole stared at her, his gaze searching and direct.

"What is it? You looked so hopeful, as though my being a world away would answer your prayers. Are you moving back to the area?"

His wry tone wasn't lost on her. "No. I've told you I like Florida." And she did, even when she was excruciatingly lonely.

"Then why so leery of me? Is it because I didn't write to you at first—"

"You didn't write to me at all," she blurted out, then looked away from him. She prayed that the music would end, that the seven-piece band conscripted from the music department of the university would cease segueing from one song to another.

"I did write. Several letters, once I was settled. I never received one from you."

That surprised her. She shook her head. "You must be mistaken, Cole. I sent you a letter every day . . . at first." Then I found out I was pregnant with your child, that I was moving to Florida, that I had no hope of supporting myself or having the child unless I relied on my folks. After that, I stopped writing.

"No, no, Del, I wrote to you, every day after I was settled."

The music stopped.

"Dance is over," Del said, stepping back from him.

"Wait, Del."

"I have to find Marge."

"I'm going with you. Now tell me about those letters you wrote."

"No, it's water over the dam and nothing to fuss about now." Frantically, she looked around for Marge. She could barely get her breath. She felt suffocated, as though she'd been underwater too long.

"This way," Cole said tightly. "She's over there." They took a few steps, then he stopped her by stepping in front of her and taking hold of her arms. "I want some answers about the letters, Del. I mean it."

"Not relevant. As a lawyer you should understand that."

"To me it's relevant. I want to know."

"You're making mountains out of molehills," she told him, trying to unhook herself from his hold. "You're more of a caveman than you used to be, Cole. Release me. I want to find Marge."

"I have the distinct impression you'll bolt if I let you go." Still, he released her, staying at her side as she continued toward a knot of former classmates.

Del felt every eye on her as they crossed the room.

"Relax, Del," Cole murmured. "I'm staying."

His cryptic remark stiffened her spine like a steel rod had been implanted in it.

When they approached the small group near the far wall, Cole's smile was easy. "Hi, Marge, Katie, Will. How are you?"

"Fine," Will Gaiter said, laughing. "I see you've got Del in tow. As I recall, you two were quite a pair in the old days."

"Will!"

"Aw, Katie. I'm not stepping on any toes, am I, Cole?"

"Not that I can see."

"How's it feel to be back in the old hometown, Del?"

"Fine, Will." She tried to smile, but it wasn't working. She stared desperately at her friend.

"Er, ah, Del, come to the ladies' room with me," Marge said.

"You bet."

"See you," Cole whispered as she passed him.

Just as Cole had picked up on, she longed to bolt from the gymnasium. Out the door, to the car, back to the house to get Laurie, then to the airport and Florida, and safety. How strange. Most of the time she'd been in Florida, she hadn't felt secure. She'd felt lost and lonely. Now it loomed in her mind as a haven. The tall, muscular, modern god with the black satin hair, gold-flecked hazel eyes, and strong jaw had become a winged specter overshadowing her life with danger. The faster she put Cole Whitford behind her the better off she'd be.

Del pulled Marge with her at a trot. The two almost ran across the dance floor to the small, rather dingy bathroom, filled with the myriad smells of bleach, antiseptics, and old covered-up odors that had worked their way into the woodwork.

"Did you know he'd be here?" Del asked, a little out of breath.

Marge looked shamefaced. "I didn't know he'd be here, but I knew he'd returned to the area."

"And you didn't bother to tell me."

"You wouldn't have come up from Florida, and I wanted you here," Marge said stubbornly. "You've been gone too long, Del—"

"And there are a great many good reasons for that. My child is in a private school that doesn't cost the earth, as it would in the North; my career, which happens to be doing very well and will soon give Laurie and me greater fiscal independence, is based there; and—"

"And Cole is here," Marge said softly.

Del hesitated. "Yes. And there's a damned good reason for avoiding him too."

"You could tell him about Laurie, Del. He's not an ogre."

"I agree. But he'd want to be near her, in her life. She'd want the same." She held up her hand when her friend started to speak. "And I think Laurie should know her father. But I can't just plummet into it. At this particular moment, I'd just as soon not tell him. I need time to get used to the idea."

"Were you ever going to tell him, Del?"

She pondered that. "Yes, I think I'd want to. Besides, Laurie thinks she has a father in California. She'd want to contact him at some time, I'm sure."

Marge nodded.

Del's smile slipped. "It was such a shock, seeing him like that. I still feel dizzy." Blood pounded through her just from her thinking about being held in his arms. No, she couldn't be weak. She had a daughter. She had to make good decisions.

"He doesn't own the area," Marge said. "We don't have to see him."

"Actually, his family used to own a great deal of land in this county."

"So does he, even more than his folks, some say. But he isn't a king, for heaven's sake, and he wouldn't lord it over you. I wouldn't let him." She hugged Del.

Del squeezed her friend. "Is his office in town?"

"Just outside, off routes five and twenty."

"Why so far out?"

"That's not far. Doc Ringwald had the same place, and we didn't think he was far."

"He has his law office in a veterinarian's clinic?"

Marge frowned at her, then turned to go into one of the cubicles. "I'd better go while I'm here, or I'll have to come back. And Cole doesn't practice law. He's a vet."

"What? He went to law school, didn't he?"

"Yes. Cornell. But his father died, and all of a sudden he was back in Cornell at the veterinary school." Marge laughed at Del's incredulity. "I know. Seems strange. The way I've heard it, he passed the bar, went into the firm, and practiced for a very short time. At the death of his father he went back to Cornell to vet school. He finished in two years. He was always smart. Then he took over Doc Ringwald's practice when he retired and went to Arizona. Built-in practice, and getting bigger. He's done a lot with his life in thirty-three years."

Del leaned against the sink. Cole was a vet. Actually, it wasn't strange. He'd always had an assortment of animals following him around his place—cats, dogs, ponies. "I didn't know."

Marge came out and washed her hands. "You never asked, so I never mentioned Cole." She gazed at her friend sympathetically. "I wanted to talk to you about him. So did Sid. We figured it was a sore subject."

Del nodded. "You always were a sweetheart. Let's get out of here."

When they approached the table where they'd left the others, Del looked around for him.

"Are you looking for Cole, Del? He left," Will said, smiling. "Seemed in a big hurry. Maybe he has an emergency."

"Oh. Sure. It was good to see him." But it didn't feel good now. She couldn't quite smother her disappointment at his leaving, so she smiled and lifted her glass of mineral water and lime.

She rose quickly when Will asked her to dance, then afterward eagerly danced with several other friends. She wouldn't think of Cole, she told herself.

It didn't seem to matter, though. The evening had acquired an aftertaste. Cole had turned it sour for her.

When they were playing the last dance, she turned to Marge. "Maybe we should go."

"Right."

"I'll drive you home," a voice said behind Del.

"Cole!" She whirled around and found herself staring at him.

"We thought you'd gone," Marge said. "And you don't need to drive us home. I brought my car."

He held out his hand. "Give me your keys, Marge. I've arranged to have someone drive your car home for you. I'll take you and Del."

Del stared helplessly at Marge.

"I should drive, Cole," Marge said. "It'll be out of the way for you and—"

"No problem." He put a hand through each of their arms and led them slowly across the floor, bidding good night to the many who called to him.

"Vets are popular people," Del muttered.

"So, you found out I'm not a lawyer," he said.

"Yes."

"I told her," Marge said, grimacing. "You two are making me uncomfortable."

"Don't be, Marge. It's just that Del and I have some things to settle. Like ten years."

"No we don't," Del said through her teeth, then smiled at another acquaintance who waved good-bye. "Water under the bridge."

He touched her waist, letting his fingers linger there. "We should talk now—"

"It's late."

"Not really. But we can save it until tomorrow."

"Tomorrow?"

"Your voice sounds rusty. Sore throat?"

"No. What about tomorrow?"

"We'll be able to talk more at the barbecue tomorrow."

"What barbecue?" Marge and Del said at the same time.

"I'm having one for the alumni and friends, at Greenmount."

"Greenmount?" Del repeated.

"Yes. I own it now. You must remember it, Del. They had the old stables there and rented out horses. You learned to ride there, didn't you?"

"Yes, but—"

"So did most of our friends," he went on blithely. "I learned on my dad's place."

Del eyed him suspiciously. "What about Greenmount?"

He led them to a shiny forest-green Cadillac, opening the doors for them, seeing them seated.

"Where did you get this car, Cole?" Marge asked from the backseat. "I thought you drove a Porsche."

"I do."

"Oh."

"Money must be good in soaking fetlocks," Del murmured.

"It is," Cole whispered back, laughing. "Marge." He glanced over his shoulder at her. "Either you bring her tomorrow or I'll come and get her, and you're to bring your army too."

"Nat and Judy?"

"Yes, and don't sound as though I'll regret it. There'll be plenty for them to do, and I've arranged for sitters, so that you can join in the fun."

"Oh, Cole, that sounds wonderful." Marge sighed loudly.

It was on the tip of Del's tongue to argue the point, to say she couldn't come. After all, Laurie should be consulted. If she didn't want to go, Del would stay home with her. Even though Laurie was nine and thought of herself as grown-up, Del wouldn't leave her alone. And she wasn't going to stand for any of Cole's high-handed dictating. "I don't think I—"

"And of course your Laurie is invited." At Del's startled look, he grinned. "I asked Will and Katie about your child. They told me her name." He reached over and squeezed her hand, lowering his voice. "It'll be a great outing for Marge. Don't you agree?"

"Yes," Del said huskily.

The drive didn't take long. Soon they were in the outskirts of the town, where the houses were newer, with good-sized lots.

Cole drove into the driveway as though he was very familiar with Marge's house. The front door flew open and Nat, Marge's son, bounded out and down the curving walk to the driveway.

"Hi. I'm up late." He grinned at his mother. "*The Revenge of the Body Snatchers* was on the late show. Judy and Laurie fell asleep, but I watched it to the end."

"Wonderful," Marge said. "Where's Belinda?"

"She's asleep too."

"Great."

"Yeah. It was great. I taped it so you and Aunt Del can watch it too."

"No, thank you," Del told her godchild, ruffling his hair, feeling Cole at her back. A river of relief filled her that Laurie was asleep. She might've come outside. It didn't matter that Cole might be introduced to Laurie the next day, Del needed the space that one more night would bring. She turned to Cole, holding out her hand. "Thanks for the lift."

He took her hand and lifted it to his mouth, turning it so that he kissed her palm, his tongue grazing her skin.

Del jumped as though he'd stabbed her.

Nat giggled, pointing. "Whoa. That's great. Look at Aunt Del."

"In the house, young man," Marge said acidly, gesturing for her progeny to precede her. "You're nine, you're up too late, and you've got too many ideas." She glanced back at Cole. "Thanks for the lift."

"My pleasure, ma'am."

Del started to scramble after her friend, but a hand clamped gently on her shoulder. "Yes?" she said without turning her head.

"I want you to bring your little one."

"Little one." It was on the tip of her tongue to tell him that Laurie was nine, about five months older than Nat. The difference was that Sid and Marge had married right out of high school, gone to the university together, and had Nat the first year. She said nothing. With luck she could manage to get out of going to the barbecue.

"Yes, your little girl. Bring her. And do come, Del. Marge won't come unless you do, and it would be a shame for the kids to miss the outing. I have ponies they can ride, and a great assortment of dogs and cats."

"Sounds wonderful," she said stiffly.

"It is." He touched her hand. "Something's up with you, Del. Care to tell me?"

"It's nothing."

"Oh, it's something, and maybe I'll find out what it is."

She felt giddy . . . and scared. Cole had never sounded so implacable years ago. Had he? "Good night."

"Night. It was a great evening."

His silky sarcasm ran down her back, goose-bumping her skin and catapulting her up the walk. She could hear him chuckle as he climbed back in his car.

Inside the house, Del leaned against the closed door, eyes closed, inhaling deeply.

"Tell him."

Her eyes snapped open. "Marge, the timing's wrong."

"He never married, and believe me he's had chances."

"That's not my business," Del said.

Marge grimaced. "Don't give me that, Del. You two lit up the dance floor, for heaven's sake."

Feeling herself flush from her ankles up, Del looked away. "Ridiculous."

Marge shook her head. "Don't start lying to yourself, Del. You've never done that. Face up to it: There're still some sparks between you and Cole."

"Sparks go out." And it had been ten years. Things changed. People changed.

"Sparks start forest fires. Think about it, Del."

Marge hugged her and Del had to fight tears. She followed her friend up the stairs to the small guest bed-room she shared with Laurie. She quickly changed into her nightgown and used the bathroom. She was about to climb into bed, when she glanced once more at her daughter. She was beautiful. She had Cole's glossy black hair with just a twist of curl, not her reddish-blond curly locks. When her eyes were open they were midnight blue, like no one's she'd ever seen, except Aunt Lena's, the black sheep of the family. She smiled as she thought of her aunt, who'd always been an outsider, just as she had. Then she studied her daughter. She was physically so much like her father. Just her skin was like Del's. Laurie tended to burn, unlike Cole, who always tanned so easily. But Laurie would be tall with an athletic build, like her father.

Would he know her if he saw her? Del shook her head. No matter. Now was not the time. She needed to tell Laurie first, then perhaps on their next trip north . . . She'd make an excuse not to go to the barbecue. Perhaps if she kept quiet until the last minute, then fabricated something, she could get out of it without Marge and her kids having to bow out too. Guilt assailed her that she would be denying Laurie a wonderful time. She shook it away. Survival for her and Laurie came first. And she needed time to figure out what to do.

Del went to sleep convinced she could manage to stay away from Cole's place.

The next morning three pairs of melancholy eyes stared at Del.

Marge said nothing.

"But you can see my position, can't you?" Del went on. "Laurie and I would just as soon remain here. We've traveled from Florida—"

"I'd rather go to the barbecue," Laurie said.

"And we don't want to go without her," Judy said, her lower lip trembling.

Del felt lower than the underside of a snake. "But—"

The phone interrupted her next argument. She was grateful for the respite, because she was running out of excuses.

Marge picked it up. "Hello? Oh, hi. Ah, I'm not sure if we're all coming."

Judy protested, and so did Nat.

Del stared at Marge, who grimaced.

"Sorry, Cole, I'm just not sure."

She hung up the phone and sighed. "I have some laundry to do, Del. Why don't you read or something?"

"I'll do the dishes."

"Never mind, Aunt Del," Nat said, not looking at her. "It's our job."

Silently Judy and Laurie rose to help him.

Del squirmed. "Look, guys, I don't want to keep you from an outing—"

"It's all right, Aunt Del. But we won't go without Laurie," Nat said.

Judy sighed and nodded.

Del bit her lip. "Laurie, could I speak with you a moment?"

"Sure." Laurie shrugged at her two friends, whom she thought of as her cousins, and followed her mother out of the kitchen and up to the bedroom they were sharing. "Are you angry with me?"

"No." Del sighed, looking out the window. "Do you recall what I told you about your father?"

"Sure. He lives in California and—"

"I thought he lived there, Laurie. He doesn't. He lives here, and his name is Cole Whitford." She looked at her frowning child. "Now you know who he is, but he doesn't know you."

The frown cleared, the eyes widened. "That's the man having the barbecue?"

Del nodded.

"And you think he'd make trouble if he knew about me?"

Del sighed. "I don't know what I think. It's just that I had every intention of telling him one day, or letting you contact him, but I met him last night and I'm a little off balance about it." She bit her lip. "We've always been honest with each other, Laur. So I have to tell you, I'm scared. I guess I just don't want to face it all right now." She shrugged. "It's been ten years. He has a life. We have ours. . . ."

Laurie nodded slowly. "I know. But someday I'd like to meet him."

Del smiled. "I don't want to keep you from your father."

"I love you, Mom, and I like our life, and I can give up a barbecue."

Tears welled in Del's eyes. For a moment she

couldn't speak. She lifted her arms, embracing her daughter when she ran into them. "You give me too many reasons to love you, Laurie."

The girl chuckled. "I hope so."

"I'll fix my face and we'll go down and try to explain this to Nat and Judy."

"It won't be easy. They've become my best friends, besides my cousins, Mom." She held up her hand when her mother began to say something. "Oh, don't tell me they're not really my cousins. I know that. They'll understand. I hope."

When they went downstairs they had to go through a long, painful explanation with Nat and Judy. Though the other two children weren't completely convinced, and were disappointed, they finally accepted the fact that Laurie wouldn't be going with them.

Two hours later Del was in the living room vacuuming and Marge was folding clothes on the dining room table. The children were out in the front yard playing. Del wasn't sure she heard the screen door slam, but she turned off the vacuum anyway, swiping at her forehead with the back of her hand.

"Hi."

She whipped around, then froze in place.

Marge rose from the dining room chair, her mouth opening and closing. "Cole," she squeaked.

He stood there in the midst of the children, his hand on Laurie's shoulder. "This is your daughter." It wasn't a question.

"Yes."

"You let me believe she was a baby."

Marge started across the room, knocking a neat pile of socks to the floor. "Nat, Judy, come with me. We're going to pack up some toys to take to the House of Mercy when we go to Rochester."

"We won't be going for a week, Mom," Nat protested.

"We'll do it now anyway." She gestured to the children, then paused, looking first at Del, then Cole.

Cole glanced at her, then back at Del. "Don't forget you're going to the barbecue, Marge. Everyone's going."

Del waited as Marge left the room with Judy and Nat.

"He'd better not punch Laurie," Nat's belligerent voice faded back to them.

"Shhh," his mother said.

"Nat's guessed how I feel, but he has the wrong target," Cole said tautly, glaring at Del. "She's mine."

"She's mine," Del said hoarsely.

"When were you going to let us know we're related?" Cole's hand slid down his daughter's arm, clasping her fingers with his.

Laurie smiled nervously. "I already knew . . . er, ah . . . I don't know what to call you."

"Daddy," Cole said through his teeth. "Call me Daddy, or Father, or Pa. I don't care."

"Well, I will, but don't get mad at my mother," Laurie said. "I won't let you do that."

Cole glanced down at her, his features softening fractionally. "All right. I won't." He looked at Del again. "I want her at the barbecue. I hope you'll come, too, Del, but either way, I want my daughter there."

Del's heart sank at the implacability of those features, the hard, purposeful glitter in his eyes. She couldn't recall ever seeing Cole so rock hard. His steellike determination would have made her shudder had she not been able to call on her own iron discipline, forged by years of forcing herself forward, making a living, scratching out an education and a career. "I think I understand you," she said coldly.

"Good."

TWO

Del got out of the car with the others, watching Laurie run with her "cousins" toward the stables. "Be careful," she called after them.

"I'll be on their trail, don't worry," Marge said, stalking after the happy, shouting children.

Del looked around, at the house and its colorful gardens, which flowed into white fenced pastures and rolling woods. Rich browns and greens melted into blue, as earth and trees touched sky. Greenmount Farms looked like something out of the Kentucky bluegrass country, except that it wasn't flat. It was hilly, very hilly. The pastures stretched for miles over rolling terrain, interspersed with deep ravines and gullies, and with fast-running streams snaking through all of it. Wildflowers, sumac, oak, and maple saplings rubbed elbows on the uncultivated, steep sides.

The house sat like a sprawling, creamy-hued rabbit, relaxed on its comfortable knoll, the dark green shutters and the terra-cotta front door like top-drawer jewelry adorning its regal form. The four chimneys were of gray and beige fieldstone, a most pleasing touch to the rambling structure.

In places the roof tilted a bit. There was a hitch in one of the post rails. One of the horse barn doors listed to starboard. But its imperfections made Greenmount perfect, warm, welcoming.

Del recalled a more tattered Greenmount, and how much she'd loved the old place. Now, with the almost complete and thorough face-lift that money was able to buy, it gave off a sense of well-being, radiating out over the pasture and the rectangular patches of cultivated fields that would produce food for humans and fodder for cattle. The house and its environs had been enriched in self-esteem with care and money.

"You always said this was your favorite house," Cole said at her back. It annoyed him when she jumped, her body arching away from him like a pulled bow. He wanted to touch her, to hold her. But at the moment, he was so bottled up with ire and frustration, and a growing elation, he wasn't sure what he'd do if he touched her in any way. He could've loved her to death . . . and berated her for hours for leaving him. The ambivalence all but choked him.

She nodded. "You've done quite a job of reno-vating," she said, still not looking at him, her hands threaded together.

"We have to talk."

She turned slowly. "Yes, we do."

He'd opened his mouth to reply, when a carful of people pulled into the wide turnaround in front of the house.

"Hey, Cole, where do we take this? We've got the games, old buddy. Boccie, croquet, golf clubs, tennis rackets, everything you ordered." Laughter belled out as much of the equipment was held aloft.

Cole turned to tell them where everything should be unloaded. When he looked back, Del was striding across the grounds in the direction Marge and the children had taken. Cursing, he started to follow her, but someone else called out to him. He stopped, glanced after her, then turned with a fixed smile.

Del was in a tizzy. She couldn't seem to get hold of Laurie for more than five seconds. Her daughter was in a whirl of excitement, darting here and there, extolling the virtues of Greenmount in a loud, carrying voice. Her cousins answered without lowering their voices one decibel. "Wait, Laurie."

Del was following Laurie, who was following Nat and Judy, to the stables, when Marge appeared beside her.

"Don't worry, Del. She's having a good time."

Del nodded, turning to face her friend. "I know. I just feel as though I'm losing control." She looked toward the stables again, and what she saw stopped her cold. Laurie sat atop a horse. A *big* horse! "Oh, Lord, Marge! She's never ridden."

The two women started to run.

When they reached the corral Marge stayed Del with a hand on her arm. "Approach her slowly, Del. I'll grab the reins and—"

"Mom, look at me. And it's *my* horse. Cole said I could have her."

Del stopped in her tracks.

"That does it," Marge muttered when several people looked around, curiosity limning their features.

"Wait a moment, Laurie," Del called out, her voice not quite steady. "Don't move. I'll be right there." First priority, get Laurie out of danger. Tear a strip off Cole right after that.

Cole appeared on the other side of Laurie's horse. "She's all right. I have her. And Meesa is a very gentle mare."

Del moved closer. "She's a thoroughbred. . . . And very high," she said tautly.

"And do you think I'd let anything happen to our daughter?" Cole didn't shout, but his voice carried.

People were watching them closely now, and openly listening.

Del checked to see if Laurie was mounted correctly, then moved around the mare and faced Cole. "Nothing will happen to Laurie. *I'll* see to that."

"So will I," he said smoothly, though his eyes glittered with ire.

"I don't intend to be the object of gossip," Del said, her hand reaching up to clasp the reins.

"I'm not embarrassed." Irrepressible, Laurie smiled down at her mother. "Besides, most everybody knows. Nat and Judy told them."

Del gasped.

"I'll sell them to the gypsies," Marge said helplessly.

Laurie looked puzzled. "What gypsies?"

"I think I'll sell myself," Del murmured.

"Mom, let go of the reins. I want to go riding. Cole's going to show me how." She leaned down and whispered, "I call him Cole instead of Daddy in front of these people."

"Too late," Del muttered, stepping back, dropping her hand. When Cole mounted a horse next to Laurie, she protested again. "I thought you were going to walk beside her. You have guests. . . . You can't leave. . . . I'll go—"

"No need. I'll handle it. The caterers are taking care of the canapés and drinks, and my housekeeper, Mrs. Glyn, will oversee everything else." He smiled down at Del. "If you like, you can help her."

Del shook her head and took another step back. She'd seen the hard-eyed sheen of determination behind his congenial smile. What was he planning? It was all wrong. The Cole Whitford she'd known was gone. Oh, there was still the smoothness, the charm, but now there was a glossy animosity she didn't recall as part of his personality, a gentle threat that hadn't hit her all at once. It had come over her like a prodded awareness. No casual implication, just a quiet promise.

Stupid. He couldn't be setting up some sort of campaign against her because of Laurie. It wasn't characteristic. But . . . did she really know Cole? They'd been intimate, she "knew" him in the biblical sense, but was she really acquainted with the person he was? Ridiculous. This wasn't an emotional, hostile takeover. Besides, she'd recognize such a ploy. The eerie sensation she'd been experiencing around him had begun when she'd met him at the reunion, not when he'd spotted Laurie and deduced she was his.

She smothered a sigh. It would be nice if Cole had been a little less intelligent, a little less perceptive. She might've been able to bluff him out of his notion of having a daughter named Laurie. "I don't want her to go very far," she said to Cole. "She's never—"

"You don't have to worry," he said. "I'll take care of her, now and in the future." Chucking at his mount and tapping Laurie's gently on the rump, they moved away, Cole instructing Laurie in a quiet voice.

"Why did that sound so threatening?" Marge smiled limply when Del spun to face her. "I'm too imaginative."

"If you are, so am I." Del inhaled deeply, watching the slow walk of the departing horses. "I can't fault his horsemanship," she said. But she had no intention of faulting her instincts about Cole, either. Even Marge had felt the negative vibrations coming off him.

"Of course not. Look at the medals he won for dressage," she said, referring to the formalized riding competition that was very popular in the area. She grimaced when Del scowled at her. "Sorry. I'm not distracting you and I wish I could. I wish I could be distracted from what I'm thinking about Cole."

"Explain," Del said, her mouth going dry.

Marge shrugged. "I don't know what's come over him. He's like an ogre clothed in velvet. Are there such things?"

"Yes," Del snapped, then relented and hugged her friend. "I'm a little frazzled. Forgive me."

"Nothing to forgive. I'd be out of my mind if it were me. Can you believe this scenario?"

"No, I can't."

"I'm your friend, Del. Don't hate me for inviting you back to Geneseo."

"I don't." But she couldn't help wondering where she was heading and why she felt such trepidation. Cole was in her life again, and she was damn sure he wouldn't leave quietly.

The barbecue was in full swing. There were pony rides, and every sort of outdoor game, including horseshoes and races for the children, and prizes for all. There was music supplied by a local group and dancing on a prefab dance floor under an open-sided tent.

Del was swamped with classmates coming up to her and swapping stories. If there were sly smiles and double meanings from some, she tried to ignore them. An indefinable reticence from others was more welcome.

Soon it would be time to go home to Florida, she kept telling herself. She could last until then.

Del was so relieved to have Laurie back at her side when they sat down to eat, she was able to put some of her worries on hold. At least until Cole sat down across from her. He waited until Laurie, Marge, and her children were involved in conversations with the people around them, then leaned toward Del. "Laurie suggested I come to Florida and live. She wants to be close to her father."

The luscious barbecue she'd eaten rose up in her throat. Del took deep breaths to conquer the sensation that she would lose her meal.

"Nothing to say?"

"Bastard," she choked.

He leaned across the wooden planks stretched over horses and covered with heavy, oiled paper. "Am I? What do you expect? Roses? You denied me knowledge of my child for ten years, refused to answer my letters—"

"There weren't any," she burst out, grasping on to the one detail she was sure of.

"There were. I told you there were."

"And I said there weren't." Had there been letters? Was Cole smoking her?

They stared at each other.

"I won't back down, Del."

"Neither will I."

"I'll live in Florida, or you can live here."

"My work is in Florida . . . Laurie's school. She's happy there."

"Then I'll move there. I'll be in my daughter's life, Del. And I won't want her just on visiting days, or every other Sunday. I want her in my home, in my life."

Del drew back at his serenely voiced demand. "And if I won't kowtow to your demands?"

"Then be prepared to fight me in court, Del. I've got the money and the lawyers to go over rough ground for a long time. Can you match me?"

"You think that's all it takes to have her in your life? What about caring . . . and nurturing . . . and the years we've shared?" She hauled in deep breaths, but nothing steadied her voice.

"What about your mother and father, Del?"

"What?" Surprised and thrown off stride by the change in subject, she eyed him suspiciously. "What do you mean?"

"Where are they?"

"Why didn't you put detectives on it?" Bitter animosity all but choked her.

"They looked for you in Florida, and even in Arizona."

Stunned, she stared at him. Her father and mother would've hated it if Cole had found them. They'd had an unlisted phone number and rarely kept in touch with old friends in the North.

Cole shrugged. "They didn't find you."

She frowned at him. "Why did you send people looking for me and my family?"

He took a deep breath and looked away from her. "I made inquiries because it seemed a good idea at the time." He glanced at her sharply. "I even asked Marge. She gave me some mumbo jumbo about Arizona."

Del bit her lip. "I—I told her that I didn't want to see you." At the flash of anger in his face, she shook her head. "I was young and pregnant, and my parents were appalled. I didn't need any more complications in my life." Not able to hold his gaze, she looked away. "They were so hurt. They felt betrayed. Not that they said that. They wouldn't. And I could tell they thought they'd failed to teach me morals, proper behavior. I did my level best to make them see that they didn't fail, but I'm not sure I succeeded." She knew she hadn't. To the day they died, her parents hadn't been able to hide their disappointment in her. "They would've been so hurt if I'd have involved you again. And you were in Japan. The timing was all wrong—"

"You could've let me make that decision, or at least be in on it. We could've discussed it," Cole said, his voice crackling like a too-hot bonfire.

She shook her head again. "My parents hated you at that point. It would've been anathema for them to accept you into their home. And I was too anxious about having a baby to fight them on anything. I sure didn't need any more upset."

His voice changed. "You had a rough time?"

"First babies are difficult, as they say."

"Were your parents with you?"

"At the birth, yes. Shortly after Laurie was born, they were killed in a head-on collision. An elderly man became disoriented, crossed the median, and went the wrong way on a one-way boulevard." She took a deep breath. She really didn't want to dwell on that frightening time. "After their deaths, I used what little insurance money was left and the small judgment I received from the other man's insurance company to arrange live-in help for Laurie. I finished school and took my CPA exam—"

"You always liked math."

Her smile was fleeting. Though she wasn't looking directly at him, she could feel his every change of expression, respond to every nuance in his voice. "Yes. I work in a small firm—Haaskel, Bryan and Peters, that's us. I can support Laurie and myself." She risked looking at him. "What would be the sense of disrupting Laurie's life now?"

Cole shrugged. "I don't think I'd disrupt her life. And now she can have a choice. Living in Florida or here."

Despite the unusual heat of the day, Del felt chilled. "What do you mean?"

"Just that she doesn't have to remain in Florida. She

could live here. We have good schools in this area, and she loves the farm and the horses."

Del sensed his implacability once more. "I have to think about it. It's not something I can just do. It's her life." And Del's own. She couldn't be separated from Laurie. Is that what Cole was inferring?

"We'd marry, of course."

Her head snapped up. Her heart plummeted to her shoes, then back up into her throat. "And just how do you figure that?"

His smile was twisted. "Look, Del, I want to be with my daughter all the time. Marriage is the only way."

"Even Superman would be astounded by your leaps and bounds," she said tartly. "They boggle the mind." She was trying to stay on keel, but her whole world had just tipped dangerously. Marriage! Words fought their way up her closed throat. "You're not thinking this through—"

"And you're talking like a CPA to a client who's about to be audited by the head of IRS."

"And you're being foolish. We haven't seen each other in years, we lead diverse lives, live in different states. . . . It's unthinkable."

"It isn't," he said tightly. "It's that way, or I just move in with you."

"You can't do that," she snapped. "I say who I live with, who spends time in my house. No one else." Having him in her house? Every day? Her pulse threatened to break through her skin.

He nodded slowly. "So you do, so you should. But I want a say in my daughter's life. I want to be her father. I want her to have Greenmount one day, to ride beside me over the hills." He looked beyond her. "Right now I have to see to my guests. But we'll talk further, Del. I want my daughter in my life. Remember that."

Del shivered when he strode away from her. There was that look again. It went beyond anger, frustration. It was as though he hated her. She bristled at the unfairness of it all. She hadn't abandoned him. She was the one who'd had the child alone, who'd struggled to get on her feet. She felt foolish and petty, threatened, disconnected, off balance. She walked toward the stables rapidly.

People spoke to her. She supposed she returned their salutations, but she was so undone she couldn't be sure of anything.

How could she handle it? If she went along with Cole she was sure to leave herself open for some world-class pain. If she fought him, she could lose Laurie. He had the money, the power to thwart her. Did she have a choice? She had to make sure that Laurie's life was right, that it was as normal as possible.

Normal? Would anything ever be normal again? It wasn't normal for her heart to be fragmenting in her chest, or for acid anger to be burning her guts. Damn you, Whitford!

* * *

Later in the day another meal was served. Just looking at the food made Del's uncertain stomach turn over.

She was dumbfounded as she watched her daughter wolf down huge slices of watermelon, then tackle a small steak, and a small drumstick, along with macaroni salad and homemade potato chips. "I've never seen her eat cucumbers before, Marge."

It wasn't her friend who chuckled at her back.

Del turned, gazing warily at Cole. "It's just that she can be picky about food. Today she isn't."

"I had an appetite like that when I was a youngster." He touched her arm. "Something bothering you?"

"No."

"Yes, there is, but you're not going to tell me about it. Someone make a remark about *our* child . . . or *us*? Or was it our earlier conversation?"

She ignored his questions. "You still have a big appetite. I saw your plate." She could've bitten her tongue when he guffawed.

"Watching me again?"

"No!" she snapped.

Laurie finished, swiped at her mouth, then asked to be excused. In seconds she was racing after her cousins, who were cavorting out on the dance floor. Del rose to go after her daughter, but Cole stopped her.

"No, leave them alone. We'll dance by them."

Before she could respond, Cole swept her into his

arms, leading her in the fast country two-step the fiddles and the guitars were hammering out.

She'd forgotten country dancing and how much she'd loved it, those few times they'd gone for hayrides in the fall, then danced in the barn for long hours after that. Clutching Cole's shoulder, surprised laughter belling out of her, she gave herself over to the unalloyed joy of dancing.

"Look, it's my mother," Laurie said, laughing.

"And your dad," Nat bellowed.

"Nathan!" Marge shouted to her son, shaking her fist.

Del didn't even wince. They all knew anyway. In a town like Geneseo, news hummed through the air like a fiber-optic reaction.

"I can feel you putting up your shield," Cole said. He was bent over her, speaking into her ear so that she could hear him over the exuberant playing of the musicians.

"What do you mean?" Del had a fluttery sensation as she was forced to speak too closely to his ear. Damn him for making her aware of him. No doubt he had a stable of women. She pushed against him.

He frowned down at her and held her tighter. "Take it easy. I meant that I'm sure Marge and I weren't the only ones who heard Nat."

Del nodded, shrugging slightly.

"No comment?"

"None." But her insides roiled with reaction to his

look, to Nat's comment, to the speculative stares of some of the guests.

The music stopped abruptly. They were in the middle of the floor.

"We're taking a break, folks. Be back after we quench our thirst," the leader of the quintet shouted, to the groaning protests of the dancers and onlookers.

When Del would've moved away, Cole took hold of her arm, sliding his fingers down to clasp hers. "We might as well look like her parents."

A parent! She felt less like a parent than she had since Laurie's birth. She felt like a gauche, unfledged girl . . . much as she'd felt when she'd dated Cole those long years ago.

"Hey, Cole," a man called to him as they left the dance floor. "The food was great. My kids never had such a good time."

"Well, I hope you're going to stay longer, Ray."

"Can't. Two of mine are out on their feet. Mindy says we should go. Thanks again." Ray Carter's gaze slid to the clasped hands, then up to Del's face. "I remember you, Del, though you were a few years behind me. I used to watch Cole act like a day-old colt when you'd show up."

Del laughed, surprised that she didn't feel embarrassed. When she looked at Cole, her jaw dropped. His face was crimson.

Ray chuckled. "Cole never liked it when we'd josh him about you."

"Didn't he?" Del was intrigued at the way Cole's color deepened, how, though his company smile was in place, a small tic jumped in his cheek.

"No, he didn't. Well, I just wanted to say thanks, old buddy. Coming out to look at my mare?"

"I'll be out Monday, but I'm going to let Bill Kincaid take over my practice for a time. I'm planning to stay in Florida."

Del jumped as though she'd been stung, though May was early for wasps.

"Oh? How come, Cole? It's getting on for nice weather around here. You don't want to be in Florida." Ray grimaced. "Sorry, Del. I forgot you lived there."

"That's all right. It does get very hot in the summer." What did Cole mean? she wondered in alarm. She'd expected he wouldn't come to Florida until at least the fall. They stood together watching the Carters get into their Voyager and tool down the long driveway to the access road.

"About Florida—" she began.

"I'll be joining you there," he interrupted. "If you don't want me at your place, I'll get a hotel."

"But . . . but I'll be working. Laurie will be in school—"

"I figured that. It's only May. She won't finish until the end of June. Right?"

Del nodded. "What will you do all day?"

His smile twisted. "I'll find something."

THREE

Florida was hot. Without air-conditioning Cole would have sweltered. He'd been there almost three weeks. They were well into June, almost time for school closing, but it felt like the middle of August to him. The bugs drove him crazy. The atmosphere was so heavy, he panted instead of breathed, or so it seemed.

He hadn't been so happy in years.

Each day he became more in sync with his daughter. More and more he realized how much he'd missed in not being with her since her birth, not watching the changes as she grew. He couldn't call back those times, but he fully intended to make up for the loss of them.

His built-in resentment of Del, which had erupted when he'd spotted her at the reunion, took on a new hardness. Reason told him it was wrong to blame her for the lost years. She'd been young, scared. Her parents had been ultraconservative and punitive. After

Laurie's birth she'd been alone, with no friends, frightened. Over and over the arguments presented themselves, but they didn't calm his burgeoning anger.

He wanted a knock-down-drag-out fight with Del. He wanted her hurting as he'd been hurt. All those years he'd searched for her, wondered about her, asked her friends about her. And she'd told them she didn't want to see him. It was irrational after so many years, but he couldn't tamp down the hot ire, the boiling need to let her know how hurt he'd been by her rejection. And she certainly couldn't have been alone all that time. Had she chosen another man to be Laurie's father? Her lover? No way he'd let *that* continue!

They'd battle it out, if need be, but he wasn't about to let anyone usurp his place with Laurie . . . or Del.

Cole wasn't small-minded enough to provoke a quarrel with Del just to relieve some of his vitriol. Still, he couldn't ignore his resentment, either. He had to vent it some way. It still shook him to recall the moment he'd seen her at the reunion, near the dance floor, conversing, laughing.

At the sight of her, old emotions, long buried, had flooded through him. He'd recalled, so clearly, his desperate search for Del, the phone calls he'd made from Japan, his failed efforts to find any trace of her or her parents when he returned to the States.

He certainly hadn't expected to see her at the reunion, her tenth, his fifteenth. In fact, he hadn't even planned on attending. Will had pushed him to go.

The wheedling for the heavy donation for decorations had taken less time than the arm-twisting to attend.

Then there she was. For long moments he'd only stared, trying to mask his shock behind his beer mug, to smile and make small talk.

When he'd finally pulled himself together enough to approach her, his heart had thumped so hard in his chest, it hurt. And though she'd appeared surprised to see him, she hadn't seemed to be as poleaxed as he. That ate at him.

And his beautiful daughter! He would've known her anywhere. She was the image of himself at that age. Anyone who thought girls looked like their mothers hadn't seen Laurie and him side by side. And he was so damned proud of that, he could bust apart. Yet there was so much of Del in Laurie. The mannerisms, the laugh, the habit of hugging herself when she was pleased, the way her eyes would widen when she saw something wonderful. She had all Del's winning ways. Damn Del!

He pulled into Del's driveway, put the rented car in park, then leaned forward, his forearms on the wheel. It was a small ranch-style house on a postage-stamp-sized lot, cheek by jowl with its neighbors, as were many of the houses in that neighborhood of Orange City. He'd rented a condo in Orlando. It wasn't a bad drive, but he would have been happier closer to Del and Laurie. The condo belonged to a friend from law school who had a corporate practice based in New York City, but who handled corporations in burgeoning Orlando as well.

The front door burst open and Laurie jumped down the one step, running to the car. "Hi, Dad. Guess what? I have only half a day of school today. Mom promised me she'd take the afternoon off. I want to go to Epcot Center." It was all said in a rush of words followed by a big smile.

Cole climbed out of the car, grinning. She was a beautiful child, healthy, happy, and darned well adjusted from what he could tell. "That's wonderful. I'll pick you up at school."

Laurie grinned. "You'll have to call and get permission. Otherwise I'll have to go on the school bus."

"I'll get permission."

She laughed, then scanned the street and grimaced. "Gotta go. There's the bus." She turned around, throwing herself at him and hugging him, as she'd been doing almost since their first meeting.

Cole hugged and kissed her, then watched her run to the bus, get on, and wave before the door closed. He stayed where he was until the vehicle was out of sight. When he turned around, Del was coming out the door, briefcase in hand.

He intercepted her on the walk. "I'll drive you. Then I can pick you up after I get Laurie. I'm looking forward to seeing Disney World." He could see her bristle and hid a smile. Hell, if she thought he wasn't

going to take advantage of seeing Laurie every minute
he could, she was dead wrong. And it tickled him to see
her prickle at his words.

"And are we doing that?" she asked.

"We are." He fought another smile when her mouth
pursed up. "You look like Miss Phipps." He knew she'd
react to being compared to the high school's dried-
prune librarian, who'd never said anything but "shhhh."
The sibilant sound had been as much a part of her as
her sour facial expression.

"Whaa-at?" Stupefied, Del stared at him, a reluctant
laugh bubbling up in her. "I couldn't look like that."
She conjured up the image of the steel-spined martinet.
There'd always been a contest to see who could imitate
the renowned frown the best. A startled giggle burst out
of Del. "Of all the insulting—"

"I can't help it. You looked like this." He screwed
up his mouth.

Her nervous chuckle became a full-blown laugh.
Del stared up at him. He was so tall, his shoulders
so broad. His hair was cut short, but a little longer
than some. The streaks of gold through the ebony
gave it a russet cast. The traces of gray at the sides
made him even more attractive, though he didn't need
any help. His tall, rugged good looks had always been
as casually worn as old slippers, but there was nothing
homey about his sex appeal. It came off him in exotic
waves.

Who was his current love interest? She hadn't

needed Marge to tell her that women chased him. Hadn't they always? She recalled being awed that he'd chosen to date her. That memory made her squirm. When she'd been young she'd thought him beautiful. She'd been a silly child. Now she knew he was just alarmingly attractive. "I should go," she said.

Cole looked down at her. Her nearness made him forget his enmity. He wanted to talk with her, connect with her. Maybe the painful years of wondering where she was, what had happened to her, would always be in the way, but there was an elusive magnet that pulled him to her. Laurie. That had to be it.

"I thought I'd forgotten you until the night of the reunion." The words were out before he realized he'd said them aloud.

Del stared up at him.

Neither moved.

Cole didn't want to take a breath.

Del shrugged helplessly.

"Del, don't . . ." His voice trailed off, and he turned to open the passenger door.

Del held back for a moment, then entered his car. She watched as he crossed in front of the vehicle. Their eyes met. His face was twisted with a hidden emotion. Rage, she wondered, or sweet memory? Had she ever known him?

He got behind the wheel, but he didn't start the engine right away. "We have to come to some sort of agreement, some common ground."

Del stiffened. She turned slightly on the seat to face him. "I thought that'd been done, that you're down here because of it."

He shook his head. "I see my daughter every day, but I'm not with her. I want that." He looked at her. "Are you involved with a man?"

She hesitated, watching him warily, wanting to lie. "No. I date now and then, but—"

"Good. I'd like you to think in terms of something permanent between us."

Del shook her head, even as her heart pounded out of rhythm. With an effort she forced her mind to focus on mundane things. "Could we talk on the way? I have a nine o'clock appointment."

"Sure."

They drove for long flat miles toward her office in De Land. Words conjured up soundlessly between them. Bouts were fought with thoughts. Lives were juggled with voiceless opinions.

"Well?"

Del took deep breaths. "We've discussed this before—"

"And I want an answer."

"I guess you'd better spell it out again." She hated the squeak in her voice. Was her life tilting out of control? No! She wouldn't allow that.

"Something legal," he said, "that would give me my daughter and a down-to-earth home life."

"Go on." But she knew. Every pore of her skin was

alive with the answer; her head and heart throbbed with it.

Cole stared out at the clotted traffic. "Marriage."

The world not only tilted, it spun. No mention of love, desire, hope, togetherness, trust. Such a union could be a hell-begotten mess, a lost continent devoid of communication and caring.

"I want a life with my daughter. I don't want a half-life for her where she's split up on holidays between parents. Children survive that, but it's not the healthiest way to raise them."

"I agree. But Laurie and I have been happy. We share things—"

"I don't doubt that for a minute. And I want to be part of it." He signaled for a left turn and pulled into the small parking lot adjacent to the building that housed her business. "Think about it, Del. I'll pick you up at eleven-thirty, then we'll go back and get Laurie at school. It's on the way to Orlando."

Just like that, he'd planned the outing to Orlando. Takeover artist! "Fine. I'll have to switch and cancel a few things, but it can be done."

"I know. Laurie said you'd take the afternoon off."

Del bit her tongue. She didn't look at him, but she could feel him smile. For two cents she'd punch him.

She deflated like a punctured tire. Why fight it? She did want a good day for Laurie. Her daughter talked of Cole all the time, and she seemed to exult in sharing with any and all the news that she had a father and that he wanted to be with her in Florida. She hesitated, then said, "I think we'd have to discuss this situation thoroughly before it's ever broached to Laurie."

"I agree. What do you want to know?"

She clutched the handle of her briefcase. "This marriage. Is it to be a real one, or some sham that we act out for Laurie?" She had no intention of entering some quasi relationship where they each went their own way, and only got together for occasions involving Laurie. That could be as destructive as nothing, and not just for Laurie.

Cole noted her white-knuckle reaction. His own hands tightened on the wheel, and his foot slipped off the brake. The car bumped ahead before he stopped it again with a jerk. "A real marriage. I'd like more children. What do you think?"

Without love. The words rang in her head. Del unfastened her seat belt. "And what if we end up hating each other?"

Cole was around the car before she could open her door. "We won't let that happen."

She stepped out. "You're not a miracle worker, Cole. Resentments, old and new, will rear their heads. We'll react. Without love, it could get pretty abrasive and destructive." She turned and walked away.

He watched her, hands clenching and unclenching. No love. That's what the woman had said. "I want to try, Del," he called after her.

She paused, but didn't turn. Then she strode into the building.

*   *   *

All morning Del agonized, reasons jangling around in her head like marbles in a bucket. Why should she marry Cole? A hundred reasons. Why shouldn't she marry Cole? A thousand reasons. It was like having the flu. She was racked with cold sweats of the mind, fever of the spirit, chills of the heart. And no reasonable prescription presented itself. She could be unwell forever. Lord, her head hurt. She managed to mislay one client's file and misplace documentation on another's. Would anything ever be right again?

Disney World opened to them like a morning glory in the still early afternoon, after they'd driven through a veritable labyrinth of beautiful hotels and motels to the parking lot of Epcot Center. Laurie was all but jumping out of her skin in excitement.

"Why hasn't she ever been here?" Cole asked Del while the trio waited for the trolley that would take them from the parking lot to the entrance.

"She's been to Magic Mountain," Del said defensively. She'd worked night and day to break even with the world. Epcot Center was a luxury. When she'd tossed a coin over what her daughter could and could not have, luxuries were at the bottom of the pile. But she'd managed the tickets for Magic Mountain the year before when Laurie's Class Day had featured a trip to Disney World. It had been worth every penny—Laurie had raved about her day for quite a while after that.

"I see." Cole helped Del on board the tram. As they rode through the warm, moist air to the bank of gates, he considered her hesitation, her tone of voice, and his eyes narrowed. "You've had it rough a time or two, haven't you, Del? I mean financially."

She shrugged, not able to stem the rush of heat up her face. Cole was too bright for his own good. She wasn't sure why it hurt to have him know that she'd struggled to send her daughter on an outing to Disney World, but it did. "Others are worse off, and Laurie was never unhappy."

"I know," he said softly.

She shivered with a mix of dread and delight, positive that more time with Cole would take her sanity.

From the moment they pushed through the turnstiles, Laurie was enraptured. "Look," she breathed, clapping her hands in glee.

Cole looked at Del and smiled. In unspoken agreement, their previous discussion was put on hold. Their daughter's joy would be the focus.

"Where first?" Cole asked Laurie, who was bouncing around like a Mexican jumping bean.

"I don't know, Dad. All of it."

They decided just to move to the right, traveling slowly from pavilion to pavilion, examining all the wonderful treasures of each one. Then they went around the lake to view the international pavilions, stopping at the French one for a snack.

Del ate her croissant and drank her café noir with more appetite than she'd had since the reunion and her first sight of Cole. She was balancing her life on a high wire, and she was wobbling. What was worse? Cole staying? Cole leaving? Her whole existence was in a state of suspended animation, emotionally and mentally. And she could feel him watching her as though he could read her mind.

They trooped and trooped through the Center, until they'd seen a great share of it, although certainly not all.

When they were sitting on a bench sipping lemonade, Laurie asked if they could go to Magic Mountain.

Del bit her lip. "I don't know, honey." It would be rough to fit it all in in one afternoon.

"Don't worry," Cole said. "I've covered it. I've bought tickets for everything. We'll have dinner first. Then we'll rest. Then we'll go to Magic Mountain."

Del looked skeptical. "It's a long drive back for that. And Magic Mountain isn't open as late as Epcot."

"I've taken care of that too."

Del, on the verge of replying, looked at her daughter.

Laurie was jubilant.

"How?" Del asked weakly.

"You'll see." Cole grinned when Laurie whooped.

"A surprise? I love surprises. Don't you, Mom?"

"Oh yeah." Del grimaced as Cole laughed.

They left Epcot and drove the circuitous route to the Grand Floridian Hotel. As Cole parked the car Del stared at the beautiful replica of resort living at the turn of the century. The buildings, with their red roofs and white facades, were strikingly elegant.

Cole gestured to Del and Laurie when they hung back. "They expect us."

"Here?" Laurie was dumbfounded. "Wow. It's so beautiful."

"Are you sure?" Del's heart thumped at the look in his eyes. Sometimes the Cole of long ago showed through: levity, kindness, a gentle teasing that warmed the soul. She saw that younger Cole now. She loved it, but it didn't totally relax her.

"I'm sure." He grinned, taking her elbow and gesturing to Laurie to take his other hand. "We're a family. Didn't you know?"

They stepped inside the spacious lobby, pausing to drink in the splendor that really belonged to the time of the Vanderbilts and Rockefellers. Opulence, silent but obvious; old money, grandiose and grand.

Cole strolled over to the desk while Del and Laurie gawked. When he walked back to them Del immediately saw the key in his hand.

"Don't tell me we have a room here," she said.

"We do. In fact, we have a small cottage. We'll get

room service, put our feet up for a while. When we're rested we'll go to Magic Mountain. Now that the days are getting longer we'll be able to see everything."

When he took her arm, Del couldn't quell the shiver that went through her. He glanced down at her. The smile that touched his hard lips seemed to tell her he knew exactly what she was feeling.

"Relax," he whispered as he guided her across the lobby. They walked out onto a wide lanai overlooking the Seven Seas Lagoon and beautiful greensward.

"We're over there." He pointed to a small house, white with a red roof that would give a view of the lagoon.

They walked down a stone walk, curving and lined with blooms.

Cole unlocked their suite and stood aside. "Enter, ladies."

"Wow, Dad, it's great." Laurie jumped up and down, clapping her hands.

Del couldn't believe her eyes. The suite overlooked the Seven Seas Lagoon. She stared out the long windows to the narrow terrace and beyond. "It's lovely."

"I wanted you to like it." His mouth brushed her neck as he walked behind her.

Del melted even as panic flooded through her. She should move, she told herself, but her feet were glued to the floor. "Thank you," she said huskily.

"You're welcome." He kissed her ear, one arm sliding around her waist when she trembled.

"Mom, you should see the bathroom." Laurie bounced around the suite like a rubber ball. "I wish I could take a shower," she said, "but I don't have any other clothes."

"Take a shower and tell me your size." He repeated what she said, then strode to the phone. He talked for several minutes and hung up.

When Laurie went into the bathroom, caroling that she was going to use the hot tub, Del turned to him. "You shouldn't spoil her."

"I couldn't if I tried. She's too decent, Del."

"Yes, she is." Del's smile trembled when he walked over to her, and took her hands in his.

"Well?" he said.

She stared up at him. "I—I think I'll take a shower. Although I don't have a change of clothes either."

"You do, if you want to wear them. I ordered some things in your size. Seven, isn't it?"

She struggled against the river of annoyance. "Very good on women's sizes, aren't you?"

"Actually, I'm better with udders and fetlocks, but I manage."

A reluctant laugh broke from her, but anger chased in its wake. He couldn't cover up his philandering! Philandering? Where had that archaic word sprung from? And what he did wasn't her business. Right?

"What's wrong?" he asked.

"Nothing!" For the first time in many years, Del could feel her control slipping. She wanted to break something. Cole's skull came to mind. "Doesn't it hamper your social life to be down here?"

He grinned, releasing one of her hands to stroke her hip. "There're plenty of people in Florida. And I've met a few."

His laconic answer didn't set well with her. She slapped his hand away. "Lucky you." Oh, for a shovel she could bash him with. She'd never considered herself bloodthirsty, but at that moment, the thought of doing him an injury gave immense satisfaction.

"You needn't share Laurie's bathroom," he said. "There's another one with a hot tub." He pointed to the far side of the living room.

Del hesitated. She looked down at her wrinkled clothes, with the ice cream spot on the jeans. "I can sponge my things off and wear them—"

"Don't be ridiculous. It won't cost you anything." His smile twisted. "And I won't expect a reward."

"Good," she snapped. "You wouldn't get one."

Even as she was closing the bathroom door of the master bedroom she could hear his laughter. Aching to smack him, she slammed the door, then began disrobing, tossing her clothes every which way. Sighing, she then spent a couple of minutes retrieving them and trying to press the new wrinkles from them with her hands.

Damn him! She'd wear her own clothes. She didn't need anything he'd purchased. How many women had he bought clothes for? Sexy clothes made of clinging fabrics, low-cut, see-through. Damn!

Ignoring the hot tub, Del stepped into the shower cubicle, which was formed by an S curve of glass bricks in place of a shower curtain. Blasting the water over the top of her, she sighed deeply. On the side of the enclosure was a small shelf holding shampoo, soap, conditioner, and a loofah sponge with a long handle. It felt so good to scrub her body and head to rid herself of the day's grime and some of her frustration.

She took her time, laved herself over and over again, scrubbed her head a couple of times.

Finally she took a deep breath, rinsed herself, and used lotion on her wet body. She reached for a towel, then pulled back. What a fool. She'd left the towel around the corner of glass bricks on the long dressing table. Moving out of the enclosure, she strolled to the dressing table. She was about to lift the towel from it, when she heard a splash.

"You were always a charmer, Fidelia," Cole said behind her.

She swung around, forgetting her nakedness in the thumping anger his caressing tone had evoked. "Voyeur."

"Darling, I can't help it."

His sarcasm exacerbated her irritation. "What are you doing in here?"

He slipped down in the swirling water. "Using the hot tub. I thought you wouldn't mind since you were in the shower."

"You thought wrong." Stiffening with ire, she faced

him, ready to haul him out of the tub if he gave her any lip.

Cole straightened, his eyes not leaving her. "Sorry. Didn't mean to disturb you."

"Disturb me? Are you out of your mind? Of course you disturbed me. I was taking a shower. You knew that." She glared at him, daring him to argue with her.

"An honest mistake?" he said, starting to laugh.

"Bull."

"Maybe to relax in the hot tub . . . or irritate you?"

The steamy heat in the bathroom only fueled her fury. "So. You admit you did it to annoy me?"

Cole tore his gaze from a lazy study of her torso. "Admit it? What? Oh sure, if that's what you want."

Del was disarmed by his casual manner, his offhand tone. The lout was staring at her. He didn't have the manners of a . . . *Yipes!* The realization was like a cold waterfall: She was naked. "Damn you! Don't you stare at me." She fumbled for the towel, then swathed it around herself, feeling the embarrassment start at her feet and redden her skin from ankle to collarbone. "You . . . you ogler."

Cole put his chin on his arms on the side of the tub, looking disappointed. "You look pretty good for a lady who's getting on in years, not in the first blush of youth, as they say, one who has a family—"

"I am twenty-eight years old. I'm not the little old lady who lived in a shoe."

"No. You've got a sexy, curvy body, and you still have a mole at the top of your thigh right next to the most—"

"You keep your cheap remarks to yourself." Del grabbed the slipping towel, all but frothing with anger. Then she stormed through the bathroom door, slamming it behind her.

Alone in the master bedroom, she closed her eyes and muttered curses when she heard him laughing, again. Ghoul! Monster! She was almost as damp as she'd been exiting the shower. Her knees had turned to jelly. She'd get him out of her life! But how? Groaning at the unanswerable question, she turned away and grabbed her purse. Get dressed, she advised herself. And stay cool.

Twice she had to wipe her makeup clean and begin again. She had to hurry. Dressing before he came out of the bathroom was the best plan. . . .Dress? Her clothes were in the bathroom. Closing her eyes, she spun around. Opening them, she tightened the towel around herself again. She glared at the bathroom door, trying to swallow her bile. She'd have to ask him to hand her her things through the door. Priming herself to do it, she took a deep breath, glancing around the room. For the first time she spotted the spray of articles on the bed. New undies, new shirt, new summer jeans, and her Reeboks, cleaned and polished.

She fought a war with herself. To wear or not to wear? Reason won over angry pride. It made sense to use the clothing. She'd give it back to him that very evening, when they returned to her house.

Tossing the towel, she slipped on the undies and was reaching for the jeans when the bathroom door opened.

Cole whistled.

"Clod." She turned her back, trying to hide her shaking hands. "I'll finish dressing in my daughter's bedroom."

"No need. And she's *our* daughter. I'll just get my things and dress in the bathroom." He got his clothes and went back to the door. "Some things don't change. You've got a great ass, Del."

She turned and flung a shoe, all in one fluid, angry motion. It struck the closed door.

"Missed me," he called out.

"I won't always," she said through her teeth.

"Neither will I."

Was that a threat? she wondered. Or a seductive promise? The man was driving her crazy. She had to put him out of her mind, but all her good resolutions couldn't quite manage it. She couldn't stem the shiver that sliced through her. Cole was a monster one moment, a gentle father the next. She didn't fear for Laurie but she had the uneasy feeling that Cole wasn't being entirely solicitous of *her*.

Being with Cole had eroded all the smooth confidence it had taken her years to develop, the sangfroid in her dealings with colleagues, associates, and clients that had sustained her in the tough times. More than one associate had commented on her coolness under fire.

Now, it had all melted, and she felt as unfledged and unable to cope as that girl those many years before who'd faced alone the birth of her child and the unspoken censure of her bewildered and disenchanted parents. Sighing, she slipped on the cotton shirt, hazily aware that it was a coral shade that she wore often and that was very flattering to her.

What was she to do about Cole?

"Mom." There was a sharp knock on the bedroom door. Buttoning the shirt, she walked barefoot to the door. She flung it open and smiled at the beautiful young lady who seemed to be growing right in front of her eyes. "Hi."

Laurie threw herself at her mother. "Thanks for today, and for letting Dad into my life. It makes me so happy to be with him."

Silently, eyes closed, Del embraced her daughter. The thorny problem was solved. She couldn't turn her back on her daughter's happiness. Laurie loved Cole already. She wanted to be in his life, be his daughter. "Would you like him around all the time?"

Laurie shot back out of Del's arms. "You mean here? With us? In Florida?"

Del nodded, trying to smile.

"Oh, Mom, oh Mom. Really? Truly?"

When Del saw the tears in her daughter's eyes, it struck her forcibly how much it meant to Laurie to have found her father. Her doubts faded away. If her certainty was tinged with a sadness that a marriage without love was like a year without spring and summer, she thrust away the pain and silently vowed to make it work. After all, she'd loved him once.

Mother and daughter were hugging again when Cole walked out of the bathroom, fully dressed. "What is it?"

The alarm in his voice caused Del to turn quickly. "It's nothing." She inhaled shakily. "I've—I've just told Laurie that you might be staying with us . . . all the time." Acid satisfaction coursed through her at the stunned look on his face. The towel drooped in his hand, then dropped to the floor. His gaze flew to Del, then to Laurie, and back again.

Seconds ticked by, the quiet buzz of the air-conditioning the only sound in the room.

"You want to, don't you, Daddy?" Laurie finally asked. "Stay in Florida, I mean?"

Cole nodded slowly. "I want that. But I hope you and your mother'll want to come back to New York with me, some of the time anyway. Of course, I know you don't want to leave your school and—"

"I don't care about that," Laurie said breezily. "I'd like to live in Geneseo and go to school with Nat and Judy." She didn't seem to notice her mother's slack-jawed astonishment when she turned to Del. "Mom, can you work in Geneseo?"

"Well, yes, I guess I could take the CPA exam in

New York," Del said. She was reeling from the power and tunnel vision of this nine-year-old who was persuading her to throw over a life she'd scraped, starved, and suffered to get—and doing it with no more effort than it would take to swat a gnat. Del took a couple of deep breaths to steady herself. "However..." At Laurie's crestfallen gaze, she paused. "I just thought it might be better if we stayed here." She shrugged, feeling discomforted under her daughter's steady gaze. "Your friends are here, you've always lived here—"

"But I don't care about that. I love Geneseo. It's not crowded."

And Orlando and its environs were. Del sighed. "Well, we can talk about it."

"Yes, we can," Cole said, walking over to them. He put his arms around his daughter and Del and pulled them toward him. "We'll be a family, either way."

"A family," Laurie breathed, starry-eyed. "I'd like that. I wish you could've come to my softball games. I can really hit."

"I love ball games," he said, earning a wide grin from his daughter. "And though I played hardball, I used to be a pretty good hitter myself."

"I know they play softball in Geneseo," Laurie said. "Nat plays." There was a touch of defiance in her eyes when she glanced at her mother. "I like Geneseo."

Del knew she couldn't throw a wrench in the works. Gazing up at Cole, she caught the glint of triumph in his smile, and she bristled. A knot of anger began to grow. He'd come late into Laurie's life, but no matter what claim he had on his daughter, he had none on her. And she'd let him know it. She'd charted her own destiny for years. She had no intention of changing now. "We can settle the details later. I thought you wanted to see Magic Mountain, missy." She forced a smile, burying her trepidation. It would rise quickly enough anyway; she didn't need to give it a boost.

"Let's go," Laurie said enthusiastically.

Cole gestured for Del to precede him.

She felt his gaze like a knife between her shoulder blades.

As they walked up the narrow winding path to the lanai and the lobby, Del's skin crawled with an awareness of Cole. Every time she looked at him, his gaze was on her. She all but ran across the lobby. What was on his mind? He didn't love her. He was marrying her to gain his daughter full-time. She could understand that. But how would they deal with each other? Life could be a desert without communication. And love was the great communicator. Her heart squeezed with the realization of lovelessness, but she was used to that. Her parents had been expert tutors.

The drive to Magic Mountain took longer than expected because of the increase in traffic that warm evening. Soon school would be out and the influx of tourists could triple or quadruple.

Laurie grimaced when they finally parked and walked to the entrance. "We won't have much time."

"We have tomorrow," Cole said easily.

Del stopped in her tracks, shaking her head. "No. I have work. Laurie has school and—"

"She doesn't. Tomorrow is Class Day. The children can attend or stay home. I talked to Laurie's principal, and she said it's up to Laurie." Cole grinned when his daughter whooped and turned a cartwheel on the tarmac.

"Laurie!" Del was caught between irritation at Cole and entrancement at seeing her serious daughter so carefree.

"Isn't it great? Say we can stay, Mom. Please."

"Your heavy time for taxes is past," Cole said.

"True," she said. He was railroading her, maneuvering her as though she were one of the stock he tended at his clinic. "I'll think about it."

As though he read her exasperation loud and clear, he grinned. "Let's go."

They crammed ride after ride into the short time they had. While they were on the simulated old-time train, which was nothing more than a modified roller coaster, Del was thrown against Cole when they went around a sharp curve. He caught her at his side and didn't release her.

"I'm fine now," she whispered.

He nodded, smiled at Laurie, and didn't release her.

When the ride was over Del felt frazzled, unglued . . . and strangely relaxed.

Laurie laughed. "Mom, your hair's standing on end."

"Well, that was some train ride. And by the way, so is yours." Del grinned at her daughter. Why hadn't she brought Laurie to the famed theme park long ago, instead of just letting her come on Class Day? Admittedly the entrance ticket was expensive, and she couldn't have done it often, but she could've managed a time or two. Maybe she'd put too much emphasis on surviving and not enough on living. She stared at her daughter searchingly.

"She's very happy," Cole said in her ear, as though he'd read her mind.

"I've missed some moments, though," Del said quietly.

"So have I."

She looked up at him, regret lacing through her as she nodded.

"No more," he said.

Del sighed. There was only one way to go. Cole knew it, and so did she.

There was a shine in her daughter's eyes, a deepening glisten of joy that she'd do anything to maintain. She put her hand on Laurie's hair, smiling when her daughter looked at her inquiringly. "I was just thinking we should do this more often." She shivered as she tried to picture the future with the three of them in it.

"Cold?" Cole took off his light jacket and put it around Del's shoulders.

"I'm fine." She tried to return the jacket but he insisted she keep it.

"Does that mean we're done?" Laurie's crestfallen face had her mother chuckling.

"No, we're not leaving. What other forms of human delight are there to see?" Del answered. There was a comfort in wearing his jacket—one she didn't want to dwell on.

"That ride." Laurie pointed, then hugged her mother. "I'll go ahead and get in line, Mom."

"She looks like you," Cole murmured as they watched Laurie race off. "And don't worry. I'll keep an eye on her."

"You know darn well she's *your* image."

"But inside of her, her mannerisms, gestures, way of speaking, are yours."

Del swallowed, running a nervous hand over her hair. "She's got your chutzpah."

Cole chuckled. "Come on, Del. We have to get in line."

She stopped. "Cole, this marriage thing could blow up in our faces. We're going about it in all the wrong ways—"

"Unorthodox, I'll admit. But methods of maintaining a marriage are as myriad as the people entering the state. And this is all we have." He took hold of her upper arms. "You don't have anyone you want to marry at the moment, right?"

Del hesitated. "You know I haven't."

"Then we'll do it, and work at it, and take it one step at a time."

Without love. Her heart squeezed. "A business arrangement?"

Cole's smile hardened. "I'd like more children. What would you like?"

Children without love. "Another one or two would be nice."

For a moment it was as though they were alone, despite the throngs of people who moved like a laughing sea, eddying around them. Then Cole frowned and looked up, his gaze sharpening on the concourse.

"We should find Laurie." He took Del's hand and pulled her along beside him.

"Can't you see her, Cole?"

"Don't worry, I will."

"Yes." She didn't pull free of him. She suspected Cole wouldn't have let her, anyway. There was a dark purpose about him that hadn't been part of him when she'd first known him, a silent force that sent out its own powerful waves. She couldn't recall him ever being so bearish, so determined.

Side by side they hurried, until they saw their girl, well back in the line, waving to them. Then they strolled, both sets of eyes on their child.

"She's beautiful," Cole murmured. "And I'd like her to go to school in New York." He shrugged. "I wouldn't have pushed it, but she did say—"

"I heard her," Del snapped.

He chuckled. "I don't recall you being so touchy."

"I don't remember you being so pushy," she shot back, then reddened when a full-blown laugh burst from him.

"I'll want to practice my profession in New York," she added.

"Why not? I could use a good accountant."

"It'll cost you."

"Wait until you see your bill when you bring your pets to me."

"I don't have any."

"Laurie will want some," he said smugly.

"We'll see about that."

"So? We live in New York?" He hadn't even realized he was holding his breath until she nodded.

"Laurie seems to want it," she said, looking up at him. "You'd prefer it."

"Yes."

Del exhaled, feeling her options slamming like doors behind her.

It had been a short exchange, but the words stuck in Del's mind, heart, and spirit. They spelled out her entire future. After that she had a hard time concentrating on what they were doing, where they were. Cole consumed her thoughts, filling all the nooks and crannies of her brain.

* * *

Later, after Magic Mountain had closed and they were driving back to the hotel, Del was all but jumping out of her skin.

The nonstop conversation between Laurie and Cole seeped in and out of her consciousness, but she took no part in it. She was wrestling demons. They were staying at the Grand Floridian, the three of them. Perfectly ordinary. People shared suites all the time. But not Del . . . with Cole Whitford. She'd only shared the backseat of a Chevy with him.

"Headache?" Cole asked her as they got out of the car.

"Not yet," she muttered.

"What the hell . . . ?"

Laurie laughed. "Mom gets like that at tax time."

"This isn't tax time," Cole pointed out.

Del said nothing, an ineffable weakness assailing her, a lassitude that had nothing to do with the warm evening or the rides on Magic Mountain. She felt not herself, but an observer of her life, with Cole and Laurie at the center of it.

By the time they reached the path leading to the cottage, she was frazzled. All the cool she'd developed over the years had deserted her, leaving behind a boneless, witless idiot who toddled along behind her daughter and husband-to-be.

"Mom, hurry, I want to watch television for a few minutes."

"Huh? Oh. Right."

Cole unlocked the door, then they were inside.

Laurie yawned hugely.

"Shall I run a bath for you, honey?" Del asked.

Laurie stared at her mother. "I took a shower before, remember? I'm tired. 'Night." She kissed her mother, then her father. "I'm just going to watch television for five minutes," she added, then went into her bedroom.

Del stared at the closed door for a minute, then nearly jumped when she heard Cole's voice right next to her.

"Have a little wine."

She eyed the glass he held out to her as though it contained hemlock. "All right."

"What's wrong, Del?"

"Nothing. I suppose I'm just digesting what the future holds. It's quite a mouthful."

"We could end up happy."

His satiric tone was like sandpaper on her skin. "I suppose."

"Why don't we look at it like that?"

She gulped down some wine. "Right. Good night." She swung around, heading for Laurie's bedroom.

Cole stopped her. "Your room's this way." He pointed to the far side of the living room, where the master bedroom and bathroom they'd shared earlier were. "There're two bedrooms," he said gently.

"Oh." She considered that it might be smarter to share Laurie's bedroom, but that would seem silly since she could have her own. And she didn't want to goad that knowing smile from Cole, either.

"The bedrooms on this side are larger," he added. "The one Laurie's using is the smallest." He threw open a door.

"So they are," Del said. She noted her clothes on the bed and entered the room. Closing the door behind her, she sank down on the bed, her head in her hands.

Rising at last, she knocked on the bathroom door. There was no response. She peeked inside, and seeing the room was empty, she stepped into it. After peeling off her clothes, she got into the shower stall and let the cold water sluice over her.

She didn't know how long she'd stood there when two strong hands lifted her clear. "Yeeek!"

"Stop howling. What the hell are you planning? Death by freezing?"

Coughing as a result of the water that had filled her mouth when Cole yanked her, she struggled against him while trying to tell him to go to hell.

"Close your mouth. I'll help you." He promptly shot water and air out of her lungs with a resounding smack between the shoulder blades. "There, now take it easy. I have you—" He reared back when she clipped him on the side of his head with the flat of her hand. "What's with you? Are you nuts?"

"I'm . . . not . . . crazy . . . but . . . you . . . are . . . if you . . . think—"

"Stop coughing and talking at the same time." His gaze roved over her. When her hand came up again, he blocked it and held it. "Simmer down."

She glared at him. "I want you out of my shower." Even as she spoke, she couldn't help noticing that he had a wonderful body. They'd made love many times, but she'd never seen him really nude until now. They'd been in the dark, with only the glow of the moon and the muted dashboard lights to see by. How had he ever seen that beauty mark of hers? In the bright light of the bathroom she looked her fill, and found him sexy and enticing. Damn his hide.

"I'm not the only one ogling now," he said. He blocked her other arm, laughing. "You're the damnedest, feistiest female. I don't recall you being such a battler."

"Survival is a great teacher."

His smile faded. "Was it awful for you?"

"Yes. No! Well, yes, at times." She tried to shrug it off, but Cole's hold on her arms prevented much of a gesture.

So there they were, blocking each other's moves, or attempting to, while they were nude and in the shower. As though they became aware of their ridiculous situation at the same time, they stared at each other, eyes wide.

Smiles began—tentative and self-mocking, but smiles just the same.

"Get out of here." Del was the first to speak.

"I need a shower."

"I'll be done in a minute." How could they be so relaxed? She wondered. They were enemies. Well,

maybe not enemies, but they weren't friends. "I'll leave."
And why wasn't she embarrassed? Since Laurie's birth
she'd never wanted to make love with any other man.
She'd concluded that Cole's apparent rejection of her
had left her frigid. Yet now she was almost frighteningly
aware of Cole. She ached to touch him.

"While you're daydreaming," he murmured, "we
could be taking one together." He reached behind her
to turn on the shower, then lifted her back into the
cubicle and joined her.

Del felt like an observer again, a person out of
touch with herself, divorced from her own personal
reality. She cleared her throat twice as the warm water
sluiced between them and over them. He rubbed soap
onto the loofah sponge, then squeezed it over their
bodies. Suds bubbled and burst on their skin, sliding
downward, creating their own sensuous path. A bubble
would pause at an intriguing point, pulling her gaze.

The moisture on Cole's body delineated every mus-
cle, emphasizing his strength, his hardness, the flat
stomach, narrow hips, the . . . Her gaze lowered, and
she began to tremble. *You fool! Get out of the shower!*
Nothing moved her from the spot. And she couldn't
stop looking at him.

She needed a physical, she decided. Mental aberra-
tions could come when a person's resistance was down,
and she was quite sure hers was in the cellar. It had been
a while since she'd had a checkup. Perhaps she was having an early menopause. Chemical changes in a woman

could account for drastic behavior. Why else would she be itching to run her fingers over that arrow of chest hair? She ached to stroke and caress those muscles. *Fool, close your mind.* She couldn't do that. She'd lost her mind. Her parents hadn't talked much about their families. Maybe this was the reason—genetic mental illness.

"You're doing it again," Cole whispered.

"What?" Her voice was more like a croak.

He leaned down and kissed her, turning her head toward him with a cupped hand. "You're wandering. And I want you here."

FOUR

Del wasn't quite sure how it happened. Did the earth enter a new orbit? Had the universe tipped?

No, nothing so dramatic or planet-shaking. She was simply turning into a wimp, she moaned to herself. Cole had turned her to jelly. One minute she was standing fast in her independence, the next she was cooperating fully in Cole's master plan for their life, capitulating without a whimper.

Not all her scathing adjurations to herself about responsible parenthood, clear-eyed adulthood, or the need to proceed with caution caused her to turn away from Cole.

It might've been easier had he not been so sexy, if he'd not been so gently persuasive, so hotly seductive. No! That was an excuse. She couldn't blame him. She was no longer a child. She wanted him. That's why she was with him. The truth of that had her squirming. She was so damned hot for him, and she could've screamed in frustration, having to admit it. Instead she surrendered.

They washed each other with fragrant soaps, laved each other's heads, slowly, surely. Despite rising passions, there was a languor, almost an indifference, to their movements that belied the heat. Rinsing was an undulating sensual experience. They were inside the tornado, and it was hard to breathe, to move, but they reveled in the growing arousal that swirled around them.

When they got out of the shower, they dried each other mechanically as they eyed each other hungrily.

"I'm not leaving you tonight," Cole whispered, as he carried her into the master bedroom.

"I figured that," Del said hoarsely. For heaven's sake, her prudent self said, she was the mother of a young girl, not some loose, irresponsible female. And she was also old enough to have a sexual encounter, she countered. But still, after all these years, why did it feel so right? She tried to deny it, saying aloud, "This is wrong."

"Hell!" Cole's steel arms tightened around her. "This is right, Del."

A stirring deep inside made her want to believe him. "Our lives have been so separate," she said as he laid her on the bed. He leaned over her, naked, his broad chest tenting her, closing her off from the world. His hot skin abraded hers and drove her wild.

"They *have* been separate, but not anymore," he whispered.

"It won't be easy."

"Most worthwhile things aren't." His mouth covered hers with insistent skill.

Her body arched toward his, her heart pounding.

When Cole felt the thrust of her breasts against his chest, need pounded through him, and he slanted his mouth across hers, taking more of her. When she thought she'd explode with the heat and wonder, he drove his tongue into her mouth, his hands becoming more demanding, ranging over her, letting her feel his need.

Del succumbed, letting the silken web of memories come alive and settle over her. She wanted him. She'd wanted him those wonderful autumn nights so long ago. Desire raged even hotter now. She wanted to drown in his hot sexuality. His mouth attacked hers with a fierce gentleness that had her reeling, needing more. When he sucked lightly at her bottom lip, she gasped, and his tongue slid through once more, tantalizing her. His hands ran over her restlessly as though he'd check every pore of her legs, her breasts, her middle, never ceasing their velvet search. Del moaned with an amalgam of emotions. She should stop him. *No, don't stop!*

His hands played over her as though she were a most precious musical instrument. Hesitant, anxious, her own hands lifted, then thrust into his thick hair. She sighed at the rich texture. Cole's hands moved just under her breasts, and she arched against him. At the movement his hands tightened, his kiss deepened. His motions were exciting, fiery. Like Cole. Once she'd thought she knew him, but there were more layers than she'd plumbed or bared. One day she might peel them back. But for right now she only needed to touch, not psychologize.

His body, hands, and mouth became more demanding, more urgent, pushing her toward the open flames of carnal love. And burn she did, her gasps and moans swallowed by his eager mouth. Writhing under him, caught in the river of hot lava building within her, Del was sure she would die. Barriers melted as her hands raced feverishly over him, trying to hold him closer, welcoming his every touch, pressing against that hot, hard body she hadn't forgotten how to love.

He tore his mouth from hers. She groaned a protest at the loss, then shivered with passion as he kissed her shoulders, her neck, his breathing harsh against her skin.

Cole knew to the second when she became as aggressive a lover as he. She strained against him, her body devoid of hesitancy, her legs fell away, parting. She was open to him in every way and it was a bittersweet reminder of times past when she'd held him and told him she loved him. At this moment it was wilder and sweeter than before, turning him furnace-hot, bringing him to a raging desire. He'd ensure her fulfillment, make her tremble with passion as he was doing. As she twisted closer to him, his heart thundered in his throat, blood cascading through him, filling him, his whole body beginning to shudder with it. Gone was the fuzzy hope of bringing her to climax again and again, of prolonging her ecstasy. Aching in every limb, he lowered himself over her, inching his way into her warm, wet cavity, his body pulsing with want as he strained to keep himself in check and give her joy.

Del had other ideas. Her body and mind longed for him, and she was wildly impatient. Thrusting upward in strong, easy moves, she elicited groan after groan from him.

He managed to keep control until her fingers feathered over his chest and she whispered, "Let it happen, Cole."

He looked down at her. This wasn't the backseat of a car. But it was the same beautiful girl, grown into a stunning woman. Those features that could tighten so defensively against him were now relaxed, flushed, her hair a curling halo on the pillow. She hadn't shut him out. He undulated inside her again, her moan eliciting one from him.

"Cole." The breathy sound of his name on her lips pushed his good intentions to hell and catapulted him over the edge.

She rose to meet his thrusts and he couldn't hold back, pumping into her all the frustration and fear he'd felt when he couldn't find her, letting his body tell her how much he'd missed her. Arms and legs fastened around each other, they rode the wild horse of passion, taking and giving, again and again. Even when the climax was spent, Cole didn't stop his thrusting motions, as though in some way he could pare back the years they'd been apart, as though he could heal the breach between them. Del went with him, her body responding in another climax, bucking with ecstasy until they both collapsed, spent, joyous, overwhelmed by the rightness of it all.

Deep inside Del was also a wavery certainty that she'd let go of more than her supposed frigidity, that she'd given away something she could never get back— a piece of herself, an important part of her personal autonomy. In the diminishing aura of great lovemaking, there was fear.

Cole woke some time later and reached for her, groggily fixing on the pillow, still indented by her head. Lifting his head, he stared at the bathroom door just as it was closing. "Del?"

"Good night, Cole."

Anger surged through him as he shoved himself up to the headboard and listened to her puttering about in the bathroom. When the light went out and she didn't return, he knew that she was going to the other bedroom, that she wouldn't be sharing his for the rest of the night.

Damn her! She hadn't changed. She'd run, gotten

herself out of a close call. There was no Florida to hotfoot it to, so she'd found a bedroom. The two-faced—

Cole shot to a sitting position on the bed, marveling at his own foolishness. His observations of Del made lies of his words. She was no deceiver. She was no coward. It had taken guts to stand alone, to raise Laurie by herself, to face those who, even in the so-called modern world, would frown on her unwed motherhood.

Why had she left him so soon after their love-making, though? What was at stake? Everything, he realized. Del was an accountant, and as such she'd factored her percentages. All had been lost to her because they'd been lovers ten years ago. She'd been left high and dry by him, or so she'd figured. Then she'd lost her parents, her last hold on a supportive world. Del was cautious. Life had made her that way. Cole felt a familiar twinge of guilt that he hadn't been there for her. He should've ignored his pride when she hadn't answered his letters and gotten in touch with her, any way he could have.

Drawing his legs up, he studied the door thoughtfully. Well, maybe he might have an alternate plan for her. And he'd make sure she was committed to the plan too. She could be prudent as hell, but it wouldn't change the outcome. They were going to be married. And he was going to teach her that the powerful emotion between them couldn't be turned on and off like a faucet. It was a potent cascade that had a life of its own, and it would stand beside them down through the years.

Satisfied that he was on the right track, Cole lay back down, plumping his pillow, a smile drifting over his face. He looked forward to the rewards, for both of them. They would be beyond belief. Hot, passionate, endless hours of love. And she wouldn't be able to run. He wouldn't let her. He fell asleep dreaming of a spread of red-gold hair on his pillow.

Del was sure her eyes weren't going to open. They were sticky, itchy. She felt enervated, filled with a lassitude alien to her.

"Get up, lazy bones."

The smell of coffee and the sight of Cole's face were a mixed bag. She needed the coffee; she hadn't wanted to confront him first thing. She had hoped Laurie would be up and about, demanding her father's attention. She hitched up against the headboard, getting farther away from him. Taking the cup with both hands, she sniffed the fragrant brew, sipped, and tried to plan an escape.

"We need to talk, Del."

"Where's Laurie?"

"Getting ready. We thought we'd visit the Water Wonders today."

His smile stiffened her spine. "Are you referring

to that lunacy of water slides and waterskiing?" He nodded. "I can't go. I don't have a suit."

"They've sent up a selection from a shop in the lobby. Drink your coffee. I'll get the suits and you can pick one." He rose and strode from the bedroom.

"Wait! I don't . . ." She was talking to air. "Damn his hide, I'm not going to let him run roughshod over me. Water Wonders! Gadfry, I'll be drowned." Pushing back the covers, she swung her legs over the bed. The short nightie, included in the assortment of clothes Cole had purchased, rode high on her thighs.

"Very nice."

Del stiffened, brushing the offending nightie down. Her face was flaming when she faced him. "Voyeurism isn't attractive."

He pushed away from the door jamb and approached her slowly, his arms filled with colorful swim wear. "I'm not usually a voyeur, but in your case I'll make an exception."

"No thanks," she said frostily, reaching for the suits. "They might not fit. I'll try them on in the bathroom."

"They'll fit," he said.

She quelled the urge to gallop into the bathroom and slam the door behind her. As it was she closed it with a decided snap, then cursed roundly when she heard him laughing.

Leaning her head against the tile walls, she closed her eyes. Life was going to be one long jousting match, with her and Cole jockeying for position. She wondered how often she'd finish on top. Picturing herself on top of Cole sent the blood cascading through her body.

She tried on four of the suits. They all fit, to her chagrin. She picked a one-piece, the sides slashed high on the thigh, the top arrowing deeply in the back and front. It was the most conservative of all of them, and provided the most cover. She barely glanced at herself in the mirror, feeling naked somehow, without armor. Deciding to don her clothes over the suit, she looked around her. Damn! Everything was in the bedroom.

The knock at the door startled her. "Yes?"

"I thought you might need these."

When he opened the door a crack she saw her clothes . . . and Cole, grinning. "Thank you." She had to open the door wider to take the clothes. His gaze dropped over her like hot coals, sending her back behind the door. Annoyed at her reaction, she reached around and all but dragged the clothing from his hand.

"Just trying to help," he said.

"You weren't."

"You've got a great body."

"You're repeating yourself."

"Can't help it."

"Would you move back so I can close the door?"

"Sure." He didn't move. "I was right about the fit."

"So you were." She slammed the door hard, hoping to catch his foot. She almost fell forward when there

was only space. The door rattled on its hinges. "Boor."
Once more she heard laughter.

She dressed in record speed, then swung open the
door. "Bathroom's yours."

"Thanks, but I'm all ready. Laurie's been dressed
and chomping at the bit, so I used hers."

"Efficient."

"If you keep gnashing your teeth that way, you'll
lose them before you're thirty."

"Trust you to notice my flaws," she said loftily,
lifting her chin and planning to walk around him.

He put his arm across her stomach, stopping her.
"I don't think they're flaws. I prefer to think of them
as challenges."

"Humph."

"Nice rejoinder," he said dryly.

As they entered the living room Laurie jumped up
from the couch, where she'd been watching television.
"Are we going now?" she asked eagerly.

Amusement burst from Del, and she put her own
fears and trepidation on hold. "Right now."

Water Wonders was as much fun as Magic Mountain, Laurie pronounced time after time. "Mom, you
were so funny on the water slide," she told Del as
they waited in line for the last ride of the day: Down
Niagara Falls.

"You were indeed, Mom," Cole repeated, and barely flinched when Del nudged him with her elbow.

"And you were so graceful?" she asked.

Cole was encouraged when he saw her slight smile. "No, but I didn't tip over and yell 'oh damn' all the way to the bottom, then get a mouthful of water."

Laurie hooted, covering her mouth. "It was so funny."

Del thought so too. And she'd had fun. She was saturated with water, and her hair hung in stringy strands. Her toweling jacket was more than damp, and she sloshed in her beach shoes, but she'd reveled in the unfettered fun, in watching her daughter duel with her father on the bumper boats and try her darnedest to best him at water polo.

Del was still daydreaming about the day as they got into the boats. Laurie was belted in front of them, she next to Cole.

"I'm glad this didn't make you nervous," he whispered in her ear.

Del shook her head. "Actually, I've enjoyed all of it." The boat was pulled up an incline and the angle sharpened abruptly. "Goodness. This is a long way up, isn't it?" She wasn't worried. It was a kid's ride.

They reached the apex, and Del blinked. She could see all of Orlando.

"We're high," she said faintly.

"Yes." Cole curled an arm around her.

"Ohhhh, Lord!" she screamed as the boat tipped downward at an impossible angle. "Weeeeee can't."

Laurie yelled with joy.

Del felt her stomach pull away from its fastenings

as they dropped straight down. When Cole clamped his arms around her, she moaned soundlessly into his chest, feeling her heart, lungs, and stomach soar out of her body.

Then they were plummeting down another watery precipice, and she clung to Cole.

"It's over, darling," he said at last.

"Are we alive?" she said into his shirt.

"Yes."

Laurie tapped her mother on the shoulder. "Time to get out, Mom—unless you want to go around again."

"Oh, Lord." She pushed against Cole, trying to climb out of the boat.

"Let me help you," he said.

"You're laughing, you beast."

"I'm amused, that's all. You were in no danger, darling; neither was Laurie. Otherwise we wouldn't have been on the damn thing."

"Hah!"

Cole held her arm while she tried to wobble after her daughter. "Here. This is quicker." He scooped her up in his arms and carried her through the turnstiles.

"Is the lady all right?" A worried attendant appeared at their side.

"She's fine," Cole said.

Laurie hopped and skipped at her father's side. "Mom doesn't like rides, I guess."

Cole grinned down at her. "Not high water ones, at least."

"Put me down," Del said limply.

When he set her on her feet, he kept his arm around her.

"I think you enjoyed that," she said to him.

"I liked the ride. I didn't like your fear."

"I liked the ride," Laurie said.

Del straightened, forcing a smile. "So did I. I guess I was just surprised."

Relieved, Laurie nodded, then asked if she could get a snack.

"Stay in sight," Cole said, reaching into his pocket for change.

"I will, Dad. Hurry, I want an ice cream soda."

"She's a bottomless pit," he said, shaking his head as she ran off. His arm tightened around Del. "Are you all right?"

"Yes."

"Forgive me for taking you on that damned thing. It won't happen again."

"Not for a while anyway," she murmured. After all, they'd be leaving for New York in a short time.

"You bet." Cole kissed the top of her head.

Her wedding day! Everything had happened so fast. How had Cole managed it . . . and her? They'd returned to New York two short weeks ago, in late June, and all of a sudden here it was, the big day.

Del had figured she'd have some time after they

were back in Geneseo. Not so. Everything had happened in a whirlwind. Her share of her business had been sold to her partners, her house had been put in the hands of a real estate agent. Cole had arranged the packing and the moving, then they'd caught a plane as soon as Laurie was done with school. And now she was getting married.

As she gazed in the full-length mirror in the master suite at Greenmount, Del was sure she was living a fairy tale. The woman in the cream lace and silk dress couldn't be her. It was unbelievable, but she was marrying Cole that very day.

The door opened behind her and a wild-eyed Marge stumbled through it. "What do they call it when you kill your children. Kidicide?" She collapsed in a nearby chair, exhaling noisily. "By the way, you look beautiful."

"Thanks. And I think they call it homicide . . . or parricide . . . or something. Anyway, you won't be doing it."

Marge opened one eye. "Wanna bet? My husband is downstairs looking for manacles even as we speak."

"They'll be good." Del tried to sound soothing, but her insides were heaving as though she'd be sick at any moment

Marge slid upward, eyeing her friend. "Second thoughts?"

"And third and thirty-third." Del laughed weakly.

"Say the word and I'll uncork one, flatten the groom, and we'll skin out of here."

Del shook her head. "I know you'd do it. I also know I have to do this." She gulped back a sob. "I'm a fool."

Marge leaped to her feet, embracing Del. "Damn, don't cry. You've never cried. Are you afraid of him?"

"Of myself," Del whispered.

"I heard that." Marge leaned back, scrutinizing her friend. "Oh God, you love him."

A sob broke free. "Don't say it out loud."

"Is that so bad, Del?"

"Yes, it is."

"Why? Because you don't think he loves you?"

"Right on the money. I know he doesn't."

"He pushed for this. That must count for something."

"Up until the reunion he was going with that gorgeous woman he'd met in law school—"

Marge grimaced. "I shouldn't have told you that."

"You didn't. Katie did, at the reunion."

"Big mistake. I'll talk to the big mouth."

"I won't be in a ménage à trois."

"Who says you will? Cole's been so attentive." Marge looked uneasy. "Of course, he always was a hunk."

"Don't tell me that." Del scowled, recalling the sophisticated woman who'd been pointed out to her on more than one occasion since her return. She sensed that Cole was important to Valerie Tighe. Then she thought of Laurie. "I'm being silly."

Marge smiled, noticeably relieved. "You are. Here. Let me help you with that veil. It's beautiful."

"Thanks. It's been wrapped away for years. Apparently it belonged to my mother's sister, Aunt Lena. She also gave me the only jewelry I ever had." Del smiled crookedly. "She was the black sheep of the family."

"In your family," Marge muttered, "that's a compliment."

Laughter burst from Del. "Monster. Maligning my family in such a fashion." As always, Marge had lifted her spirits.

"Hey, even when I was a kid I thought your parents were from outer space."

Del tried to picture her parents, but had difficulty calling up their images. "I think parenthood was too much for them. I'm pretty sure I was an unwelcome surprise."

Marge opened her mouth, then shut it and shook her head. "I guess I don't need to go into details. They're dead now. And you're free." She stabbed her index finger at her friend. "And don't forget that. You deserve some happiness, Del. Take it and don't look back."

Del inhaled deeply. "Time to go."

The ceremony was short, with only Sid, Marge, their children, and Laurie attending. But at the reception at Greenmount, there'd be more than three hundred people. Cole had overridden all her objections to a big event, citing the need to let everyone know they were married.

"Fidelia?"

The whispered admonishment had her snapping out of her reverie. "Yes?" She stared helplessly at the minister.

"It's time to repeat your vows."

"Oh." Blushing and refusing to respond to Cole's chuckle and the squeeze of his fingers, she haltingly followed the minister's lead and said her vows.

"In the sight of God and man I pronounce you husband and wife and adjure you to cling to each other for all time."

Then Cole was kissing her, all but lifting her off her feet.

"Enough, Daddy. I want to kiss you and Mom."

Cole was caught in a maelstrom. Del was his! Laurie was his! And he'd never let them go. Laurie's demand was the only thing that could've made him release Del. Reluctantly he moved back, turning to his daughter and lifting her up to kiss her.

The girl giggled. "I thought you were going to kiss Mommy forever."

"So did I," Sid murmured, earning himself an elbow poke from his wife.

"I might have," Cole said, smiling at his new wife.

Del blinked. Was that menace in his eyes? No! Certainly not. His gaze was hot, molten with desire. She felt the same wanting . . . but there was also a strange glint in Cole's eyes.

There was a flurry of congratulations and good-byes from the minister and the organist, then they were in a limousine and on their way to Greenmount.

"You're mine," Cole whispered to the top of her head.

Startled, Del stared at the others in the capacious back of the limo. Maybe she hadn't heard him correctly. When she would've pulled free of him, he tightened his grip. Leaning back, she looked up at him. "Has it occurred to you that you're as well and truly caught as I am?"

"Yes."

His lazy grin had some sort of promise, a determination in it that she found hard to fathom. "What's on your mind, Whitford?"

"You. Laurie." He looked out the window. "Ah, we're on Greenmount land."

He managed to drop the conversation by the simple expedient of getting everyone to look out the window. Del was uneasy. She was getting to know Cole's looks. Some were sexy, some were not. The enigmatic ones worried her most.

The car swept up the drive. First she saw the tents, colorful, bellying full in the stiff breeze coming off the surrounding hills. Then people came out of nowhere, shouting, waving, toasting.

"Party time," Sid said gleefully.

"Yes," Laurie said. She turned to Nat and Judy. "I can't wait to show my horse to you guys."

"Uncle Cole said we're to have one too," Nat said.

Laurie waved her hand blithely. "I know."

"Good Lord, look at the people," Del said faintly.

Marge grinned. "And they're waiting to see you."

"Did you invite the town?" she asked Cole.

"Yes," he said.

"What?"

"Just kidding."

"I don't think so," Marge said as the limo pulled up the circular drive and stopped at the front entrance to the house.

Del would've held back when the crowd seemed to surge around the vehicle. Laurie, Sid, Marge, and their children jumped out and were immediately engulfed in the laughing throng. Cole stepped out, then leaned back in to lift her across the seat and out into his arms. He laughed and swung her around so everyone could see her.

Del felt dizzy, disoriented, as people shouted at her.

"Congratulations!"

"Best wishes!"

"Look this way."

"You look beautiful, Del."

The shouts confused her, and as she whipped her head to answer each call she got dizzier than ever.

"Take it easy," Cole said, putting her down on her feet.

She shook off his arm and moved forward into the crowd of well-wishers, shaking hands, offering her cheek, being embraced. Soon she was taken up in the crush. Once when she tried to turn and stretch to see her daughter, she was all but jerked off her feet by the river of people.

"Easy, I have you," Cole spoke beside her.

"Laurie?" She had to press her mouth to his ear.

"With Marge and Sid." He glanced at her. "And if you put your mouth there again, the plans for the day may change." He held her tight to him again.

She pulled back. "Sorry."

"Don't think I don't like it, Del. I do, too much."

She stiffened. There was that sexual threat again, that almost musical nuance that ran through his voice like a velvet scythe. How did he manage to threaten her, yet make her feel so safe?

He led her through the crowd to where they were having their pictures taken, and all the while she had to fight a sense of unreality. She was married to Cole! How had it happened? And they were going to have a rousing wedding reception, by the look of it. Right-angled to the main tent was one of comparable size. Inside musicians were tuning various instruments.

"Looks like you've pulled out all the stops," she said.

"I intend to celebrate my marriage. It might be my only one."

She laughed with him, yet was deeply hurt by what he'd said. Why should she be hurt? She'd known going into it that the marriage was for one reason only—parenthood for Laurie. She had her eyes open; she could be as pragmatic as he.

After the pictures, they stood in the shade of the main tent for the receiving line. Del was enjoying herself again, until she found herself facing a beautiful, dark-haired woman about her age.

"Del," Cole said, "this is Valerie Tighe. She lives in the area now. She was married to Nate Tighe, my—"

"Roommate in law school," Del said.

"Yes." Cole looked pleased by her answer. He was about to say more, but someone else claimed his attention.

"Well, well, so now you're Mrs. Whitford," Valerie said.

"Yes," Del answered cautiously.

"You know," Valerie said, gazing right into Del's eyes, "divorce is not the ugly word it once was."

"No, it isn't, but I certainly don't recommend it as a viable nuptial choice."

Valerie's smile hardened. "Don't get too comfortable, Fidelia."

"Don't get too smug, Valerie," Del shot back, then reached out to take the hand of the next person in line. He was a distant cousin of Cole's whom she'd never met. She didn't hear what the cousin, or the next twenty people, said to her. Her brain rang with Valerie

Tighe's words. Anger, futility, and baffling jealousy raced through her like a sour flood, and she wanted to vent her spleen.

"There, that's the last of them. Now we can eat." Cole was taken aback when Del glared at him. "Now what?"

"Nothing. I'm hungry." She sailed out of the tent and almost tripped over a guy rope.

"Clumsy but beautiful. Have I told you you're a knockout in that dress?"

"No, I'm sure you didn't have the time."

"What the hell is—"

"Let's go before the food is gone."

"I'm damned if I can understand you. And they won't eat until we get there."

"Good!"

He put his arm around her waist, almost dragging her to a stop. "Now, listen to me, Del. Are we going to enjoy ourselves or are we going to carp at each other all day?"

She opened her mouth to retort sharply, but a little voice stopped her. Why not enjoy the day? They were married. Even if he didn't love her, she could celebrate being his wife. "I'm going to have a good time," she said, lifting her chin. "I'm going to dance, and sing, and frolic with my daughter—"

"And your new husband."

"That too."

"Good. Let's get started."

Dinner was excellent. It wasn't a buffet, but a catered sit-down for the three hundred guests, with special tables for children, so their parents could enjoy the peace and quiet of eating without them.

Del reveled in the broiled snapper with lemon and almond sauce, the brown rice sautéed in onions, the roasted green and yellow bell peppers, the hot crusty breads, and lemon sorbet. There were two meat dishes, as well, but she eschewed those. She noticed that Cole did as well.

Dessert was the classic wedding cake, square and six layers high, and decorated with pink and lavender roses, Laurie's two favorite colors. The silver couple atop the confection looked incongruous above the frivolous roses. When the caterer was going to make the first cut, Cole shook his head and reached for the long saberlike tool.

"We'll do it by the book," he told Del.

"I think the cake would have looked better if we'd let him cut it," she said ruefully as they sliced down the confection.

"I want a piece now," he answered.

Laurie giggled. "Daddy wants the first piece. Give it to him, Mom."

Whether it was sheer perversity, or an attempt to snatch back control of her life, or just Laurie's unconsciously provocative words, Del would never know. "I think she said give it to you," she murmured, reaching for the ragged slice they'd just made in the work of art. She turned, arm lifted, and in one fluid motion rammed the cake into Cole's half-open mouth. Gasps, sighs, and squeals from the wedding guests greeted Del's impulse.

"Del!" Marge was flabbergasted.

Laurie shouted with laughter.

Del put both hands over her mouth, horrified and tickled pink.

"Good shot, darling," Cole muttered, making no attempt to wipe the sticky mess from his lower face. Reaching out a strong arm, he caught her around the waist.

"Nooo." Del tried to pull back.

"Oh yes, princess, yes." His mouth covered hers in an electrifyingly seductive kiss that blew her apart and sent fire cannonballing through her system. She could only hang on, her mouth filled with Cole and cake, the sexiest kiss of her life.

"Look this way. I want a picture of that," a gleeful Sid called out.

"Sidney!" his wife said, irritation in every syllable.

"I can't help it, they look so cute."

"Yes they do, Uncle Sid," Laurie said, laughing, and pointing at her parents.

Cameras clicked. Camcorders hummed. People laughed.

Cole lifted his head and smiled at his guests.

Del looked up at him. "Sorehead," she muttered.

He nodded, his mouth quivering with amusement.

Del found she couldn't contain her own amusement. She shoved at his chest, laughing. "Dammit, Whitford, they're taking a million pictures of us."

"Yes. We must look like naughty toddlers."

"Hah! I never saw such a large toddler." Laughter spilled out of her.

Cole wanted to freeze the moment. He was hearing the laughter of the young woman he'd loved so much. He'd taken her virginity, and he'd wanted much, much more. Her laughter had warmed him, then fed him. He hadn't heard that heartfelt mirth in a long time. "You still have a beautiful laugh."

Both cake and amusement were wiped away by the cloth napkin handed her. Del couldn't move. Snared by his eyes, she couldn't look away. "Thank you," she said huskily.

"Thank *you*."

She flushed, her entire being reacting to the fire in his eyes.

"I guess we've given them enough entertainment," he said. "Why don't we dance?"

"Not with your face that way."

Cole braced himself when she raised her hand with the napkin in it. Her gentle swiping of the crumbs and frosting almost sent him to his knees. "Did you get it all?"

His sexy whisper dried up her voice and she could

only nod. But . . . there were more crumbs at the corner of his mouth. Whatever possessed her to reach up and lick them off with her tongue she'd never know, but she felt him stiffen, saw his eyes widen.

He suddenly whisked her up into his arms and strode toward the dance tent, his long legs carrying him swiftly over the ground, to the accompaniment of laughter and assorted catcalls.

"It's too far," Del protested, "and I'm too heavy. . . . Cole, your guests . . ."

"*Our* guests, Mrs. Whitford. Besides, our daughter is laughing and pointing along with the rest. How can I interfere with her fun?"

He reached the dance floor and let her slide down his body, relief flooding him. She wasn't as resistant as she'd been. She was cautious, but not stiff. He needed to keep her that way.

The band swung into the song he'd chosen for the first dance, and he slid an arm around her waist. Gazes locked, they began to dance.

Although she'd decided to make the most of this day, Del was surprised at how much she was enjoying herself. There was a boyish look to Cole, an eagerness that was hard to resist. Yet deep inside a voice warned her to be careful, and she knew her instincts were correct. Cole harbored a grievance, she was sure of it. Yet why would he? She was the one who'd had the baby alone. And he couldn't have married her even had he known about the baby, because he'd gone off to Japan.

"What are you thinking, Del?"

Worried that her thoughts might have been reflected on her face, she stammered, "How . . . what—what do you mean?"

"I'm beginning to read that faraway look you get. Usually you're devising some sort of plot to do me in." When she reddened and looked away, he tightened his arm. "So. I'm right."

"Wrong. You're suffering from paranoia," she said, lying helplessly.

He shook his head. "No. I read you right. Who is he, Del?"

She blinked. "Who's who?"

"The man you think of when you should be thinking of your husband."

She gasped. "You are paranoid. Did you see any man come around when you were in Florida?"

"You did admit you dated."

"Was I supposed to be a nun while waiting for you, great one?"

His scowl darkened, and he moved closer, lowering his voice. "Tell me about the other men."

Del smiled at a couple dancing past them who offered congratulations. When she looked back at Cole she was shaking with rage. "No! My other men are my secret. Like it or lump it." She spun away from him, but not before she'd seen the stunned outrage on his face. If she'd stayed with him one more minute she would've struck him. Worm! Vermin! To intimate that she was a loose woman, that she hadn't been a responsible parent to her daughter. That's what he meant. She was sure of it. She spotted Laurie and strode toward her.

"Wait." Marge grabbed her arm. "What's going on?"

Del was about to blister her friend's ear, when she noticed several interested parties moving closer. "Nothing," she bit out.

"Tell me another one." Marge steered her across the floor and out of the tent. "Spit it out."

"He thinks I'm a—a tart, for God's sake." When her best friend burst out laughing, Del glowered.

"Don't glare at me," Marge said. "I can't help it. It's so funny. You, a tart. I love it."

"I see nothing funny about it," Del said stiffly.

"Stupid. He's jealous."

Del's mouth dropped open.

"I mean it, Del."

"Why?"

Marge shrugged. "He can't count on you yet. Just the way you think you can't count on him."

"I never said that."

"No. But you feel it."

Del paused under one of the umbrella tables planted hither and yon on the grounds. "Nonsense." But she could hear the reedy uncertainty in her own voice.

"No, it's not. Neither of you are on sure footing with the other. It should make for some interesting jousting, in bed and out."

"Don't be crude."

Marge chuckled. "Don't ask me to apologize. I won't. I'm glad that someone's burning you again, that you're being brought back to life. You weren't meant to be Laurie's servant and nothing else."

"I wasn't that," Del said uneasily, wondering what the rest of the day—and the night—would bring.

FIVE

The night was quiet. Not the dead stillness of winter when snow covers the ground, but the quiet of early summer, when the birds are nesting for the night and the cicadas and crickets have yet to make their appearance.

The last guest and caterer had left Greenmount. Laurie had gone with Marge and Sidney and their children. She would spend the two days that Del and Cole had allotted themselves as honeymoon time with her beloved "cousins."

The house was so still, Del thought. Even the stars appearing in the dusky sky had a silvery silence. The moon shone shyly, waxing full, whispering its power and majesty.

Del had been in the darkened bathroom too long, gazing out the elongated window. She stared at the moon as she wished . . . for what? To be elsewhere? To be enough? To make it right?

Taking a deep, shaking breath, she looked away from the window and switched on the light. At once the garish gleam washed away the pulsating color of the night, and she was facing stark reality. Her wedding night with Cole!

She lifted the apricot silk peignoir as though it contained acid and edged it around her, shivering when her arms fitted to the sleeves, the ecru de chine lace falling over her hands. She barely glanced in the mirror, but it was enough to discern her white face, her dilated eyes, and the slight tremor of her hands, making the fragile silk rustle faintly.

She opened the door and paused on the threshold, eyeing the large room, the bed. Where was he?

"I thought you meant to sleep in the tub tonight," Cole said at her side.

She started with surprise. He'd been at the windows. Staring out at the firmament? she wondered. Were his wishes the same as hers?

"Gearing up to face the music?" he asked. When she pokered up, he could've bitten his tongue. "Look. It's our wedding night. Neither one of us is a virgin . . ."

"How apt and gentlemanly of you to point that out," she said icily.

Cole grimaced. She'd taken his comment as a condemnation for sleeping with others. He didn't want her thinking that. But more words wouldn't explain away his gaucherie. "I intend to sleep with you. Where are you sleeping?"

"Pittsburgh?"

He couldn't stop his smile. She'd always had a biting sense of humor, even as a teenager. "Sorry." He scooped her up into his arms. "Geneseo will have to do."

She tried to push against him. "You might save yourself a great disappointment by putting this off," she said.

"Oh? How is that?" He placed her on the bed and sank down beside her. The short toweling robe he'd belted around his waist gaped wide to reveal the hair on his wide chest.

Del tore her gaze from his body and studied the bookcases that lined one wall of the room. She swallowed once, twice. "I—I don't enjoy sex." At his snort, she looked at him sharply, noting the gleam of amusement in his eyes. "I realize it didn't seem that way in Florida—"

"Damn right," he said.

She struggled to make things clear. "Try to understand. That was a fluke." At his thunderous look, she inhaled shakily. "This isn't a ploy to get out of your bed. It's true. I've dated other men. You know that."

"Too many men turned you to ice?" he asked, frowning.

Slapping at his arm in unconscious pique, she glared at him. "That's not what I meant and you know it."

Her prim temper did more to restore his good humor than her words. "No? Then tell me what you mean."

She sighed. "I'm not really comfortable with this, but I feel you should know. I've had a . . . few liaisons. I wasn't . . . they weren't . . . they didn't work out," she said abruptly. "I don't think you should be surprised if the same thing happened to us."

"How informative," he said dryly.

"I'm sure I don't have to go into vivid detail."

"Maybe you do. How many of these icicle affairs have you had?"

"How many have you had?" she shot back, irked at his tone.

His eyebrows rose. "None. Mine were all hot, torrid."

She pushed herself up, eager to dismember him. How dare he tell her about his sexual encounters. He'd relish giving her the lurid details too. Insensitive clod!

Cole clamped an arm around her waist, easing her back to him. "Now wait, Del. I was joking. This conversation is ludicrous."

"Not to me," she said huffily.

He leaned down and kissed her, swiftly behind the ear. "Well, it should be. C'mon, Del. Give it a chance."

She looked over her shoulder at him. "I'm not the one playing games. You are. I was trying to be straight with you." She drew a deep breath. "I hate sex. And I've tried to like it with several very interesting men and I never . . ." Never got past the stage of taking her blouse off, she was going to say. Seeing the angry glitter in his eyes, though, she clamped her mouth shut.

"I'm not them," he said coldly.

She turned to face him. "Ah, yes, the super lover who never refuses a challenge."

"Something like that." He leaned forward. "Take a chance, Fidelia. You might like it."

"Don't be coarse." But he was caressing her inner arm with one finger, and she felt the slow, sensual rhythm in her entire body. Her traitorous legs curved toward him. "Don't!"

"What?" Cole didn't stop. Instead he inched closer, his mouth traveling the same path as his finger, his breath hot on her skin. "Let go, Fidelia." His other arm hooked her closer. When she would've protested he put his finger to her lips. "Relax. What could be easier?"

"A lobotomy?" She smiled shakily when he laughed. How could she laugh when she was going to the execution block? she wondered. Because once Cole took her, she had the sure instinct she'd be lost, and he'd lose interest, their one night in Florida notwithstanding. She'd tried to tell him that sex had become meaningless to her, that she couldn't inject any feeling into it. And she couldn't bear to want him when she knew that soon he wouldn't want her.

"This is easier," he murmured. He was puzzled that she was frightened, but he wasn't displeased. He didn't understand her fear, but he was positive she hadn't had much experience in the past ten years, despite her shaky confession about being frigid with a number of men. And he'd do everything to allay her trepidation. After all, they'd been intimate before, and it had been damn good.

"It isn't easier," she said. Still, she didn't struggle when he edged her over to the center of the bed to recline next to him. She bit her lip in hopes of stopping her body from further tremoring. "This is foolish. It isn't for us."

"We don't know that." He leaned over and kissed her chin. "I think for the sake of our daughter we should make every effort to get along, and that means sexually too. Trust me, Fidelia."

"Hah! Same old line."

He swallowed a sudden stabbing hurt. She had trusted him when they'd been together. And he'd left her pregnant, with two cold and disapproving parents, to bear a child alone. "And you've heard a lot of them."

"Some." The ragged hurt in his tone confused her.

He wasn't going to let her down, or let her get away from him, again. He'd prove they were meant for each other, and not just because of Laurie. He smiled.

Del was totally rattled. A frown, a glare, she could've dealt with, but a smile? Unfair!

Encouraged by the confusion he saw on her face, he kissed her jawline. "Umm, nice skin. And you still have that lovely elusive scent." She'd always smelled so clean, so sweet. That hadn't changed. Her hair, too, smelled the same, and was as shiny as ever. He was glad to see it out of that tight twist she usually kept it in, down and free, soft and swinging.

"I don't," she said weakly.

He kissed the crook of her elbow, letting his tongue graze the vulnerable curve. "You do. A wonderful mix of rose, violet, and newly cut grass that's both seductive and fresh as a daisy." He inhaled deeply, his nose cradled in her neck.

"How weird," she said, fighting for breath.

"Weird?"

"You make me sound like a redneck perfume." His breath on her skin had her shivering. It only made him tighten his hold. Her foolish hands were curving toward him. Lord, if she grabbed him, she'd hate herself.

"Not true," he said, his teeth nipping at the soft skin behind her ear. "You're wholesome and sexy."

"And you're a lunatic. There's no such thing as wholesome and sexy." She was boiling and freezing, trembling and stiff, giving and withholding. Insane! She opened her mouth to tell him to release her, and he kissed her, hard. She tried to swallow, to speak. She couldn't.

"Sure there is," he said. "And you're it. Wholesome and sexy." He kissed her again, his mouth lingering on hers, his tongue tracing the outline of her lips. She set him on fire. He wanted her and to hell with the world.

But more than that, he wanted her to want him. He needed that.

When his mouth moved down between her breasts, she lost all her oxygen. She wanted to tell him it was no use, that she couldn't respond, but her voice failed her. Her hands moved reflexively over him. "You can't . . . can't . . . I don't . . ."

"I can." Inexpressibly tender, he cupped her face in his hands. He saw the hint of tears at the corners of her eyes, the lacing of panic in the dilated pupils. Her shivering hesitancy was an unconscious and powerful come-on. Groaning, he kissed her, opening his mouth, slanting it over hers, taking her with tongue and teeth, giving her all the passion his hungry body could muster.

The violent passion of his touch shook her from her moorings, making her cling to him, making her arch toward him.

He tore his mouth from hers, making her groan, but she soon sighed with delight as he pushed her gown aside and kissed her breasts, his teeth worrying the nipples gently.

"Kiss me back, darling."

She shook her head even as her lips caressed his neck, his shoulders, his chest. She rubbed tentatively against his masculine nipples, feeling them convulse at her touch. An alien power filled her as she realized her effect on him was as potent as his on her, that the tremors in her body were being echoed in his. That knowledge had her quivering, trembling, but it also made her bold. She let her fingers feather down his middle, feeling those muscles tighten and tremble in reaction. Her hand moved lower.

"Wait!"

Cole's hoarse cry stopped her hand. "Why?"

"Because I'll . . . explode if you don't."

Giggles broke from her, surprising her and snapping his eyes open. The fire of his gaze moved over her. "You think I'm kidding?"

"No, but it seems a bit drastic."

"It's not. You drive me wild, wife." He'd wanted some things in his life badly, but he couldn't ever recall wanting anything or anyone as much as he did Del. For a moment, though, he was content to look at her, joke with her, play with words while the scent of potent lovemaking filled his nostrils. The vibrant beat of his heart thudding against hers made him feel strong as a bull . . . weak as a kitten. But he didn't want to hurry any of it. He wanted to revel in it all, because being with Del was the only true lovemaking he'd ever known.

His fingers slid into her thick satin hair, clasping her head as his mouth slanted over hers. "I can give you heat this way." His tongue darted into her mouth, slicing against hers. "Or I can fire you this way." His mouth slid to her ear, his tongue imitating the rhythm it had created in her mouth. "And you wouldn't have been cold in the winter without me."

"I wasn't. I was in Florida," she said dazedly. He

chuckled and stroked his hand down her spine, flattening her against his length, letting her feel how aroused he was. He looked down at her when he felt her stiffen. "You do that to me, Fidelia."

"Won't work." She couldn't swallow. Her voice was reedy and seemed to come from a great distance. He felt so wonderful. He was so beautiful.

"It *is* working." He moved against her, and felt her hips press to him automatically. When his lips covered hers, her hands fluttered over him.

"Can't be," she said, even as she caressed him continuously. In gentle persistence he pressed against her, and all the memories of his avid sexuality, his sensuous persuasion, filled her mind, sweeping her away in a vortex of emotion she thought she'd never have or want again. Her body had a life of its own. It moved closer to him, even as the voice deep inside her urged caution.

Sensation after sensation racked her at his persistent invasion of her closeted sexuality. Then, most amazing of all, heat twisted her under him, and she moaned soundlessly, her body reaching for his, the torrid response rising in her like a flash flood.

His mouth became more demanding as he felt her response, and his hands roved her ceaselessly, urgently. She couldn't control her writhing body as it tried to get closer and closer to him. Knowing that made his passion grow white hot. "I'm with you, darling," he crooned, encouraging her with kisses, sexual murmurings, love words.

The heat was making her breathless, and she panted her need. When she thought she'd lose her mind to the desire, he took hold of her breasts and lowered his mouth to them, suckling, pulling her out of herself. "Cole!"

"Yes, love, I know. Give in."

Lost in the silent, black-velvet wanting, she felt his hands slide up and down her inner thigh, his fingers catching gently on the triangle of hair and pausing. She arched her back, seeking his warm invasion, sighing when he found the damp, eager places where only he had been. Her body responded to his touch, writhing closer, desiring his ultimate claim. When his mouth moved down her body, she shook her head.

"Cole! Please."

Her ragged entreaty would've dropped him to his knees had he not been lying next to her. She'd opened to him like a rose in the morning, damp with dew, eager for the sun, and he wanted her desperately.

Gone was all hope of prolonging their love play, or drawing out the exquisite agony of desire. His own body pulsed with such need, he trembled. Sweat had broken out on his forehead; his forearms were taut with the effort to hold back.

"Please. I want you."

He capitulated because he could do nothing else, because she pulled him to her. Her words fired him so much he could only groan and thrust into her, again and again, until her cries mixed with his and the climb became a rocket ride of hot, wet passion. With a rush of emotion and love they climaxed together in a cataclysmic silence that reverberated round the room like a cannon shot.

The silence boomed louder than thunder.

Del was overwhelmed. It was as though she'd spun out of control, her body racking with the wonderful passion that Cole had engendered. She could barely get a breath as the convulsions of love continued in unbelievably serene fury.

Each clung to the ecstasy, panting in the aftermath of satisfaction, even as they each agonized over what the other thought.

Del clutched him, fearful that if she let go she'd be spun off the planet. She'd expected it to be a hot turmoil; she'd known he could do that to her. But she hadn't expected to be totally unanchored and cut loose. She hadn't expected a whirlwind that could've deposited her on the moon.

She opened her eyes slowly. He was looking down at her. "Don't say," she murmured, " 'Was it good for you?' " She meant it facetiously, as a way to get herself back in balance. When she saw the stunned anger on his face, she regretted her words, and wasn't sure how to counteract them. "Cole—"

"Never mind," he said abruptly. Hurt coiled around him like a hot wire. Had there been so many men who'd said that to her? The thought was so smothering, he had to battle it from his mind. "Are you all right?"

"Never better." And she meant it. She felt relaxed, fluid, content. Shy, but self-assured, and quite convinced that she could never have conjured up such feelings that Cole had plumbed in her. Perhaps that was the curse of being an accountant. Passion didn't compute. Sexy joinings didn't factor out. Another thought swirled around her befuddled senses, but it wasn't logical. Yet if she didn't know better, she'd have thought there'd been hurt in his eyes when she'd made her "Was it good" remark. But that was silly. She moved back out of his arms.

Cole let her go, reluctantly.

Del stared up at the ceiling. Why was Cole the only man who could make her feel this way?

Cole lay back, his arms crossed behind his head. "We have a long way to go to learn about each other."

As if icy water had been poured on her spine, she stiffened. Hadn't they just discovered a great deal about each other? Wasn't love life's greatest key? Knowledge flowed out of that. And he hadn't felt love! That they could make wonderful, sexy love together, that they could find all the erotic points on each other's bodies and fire them, had just warmed her and made her wiser. Hadn't it done the same for him? Wasn't it enough?

SIX

Del decided she was going crazy.

She needed to do something, get a job, any job, before she lost her mind. Less than two weeks after the wedding, Laurie and Cole were leading very full lives, but she was at loose ends. Not that there wasn't cause for optimism; there was. All sorts of people had come to her and said they'd like her to be their accountant, most of them close friends or associates of Cole's. But there were innumerable steps she had to take, one by one, before she could be fully licensed by the state. She'd taken the time to go over the procedures several times to insure that her licensing wouldn't be held up by some bureaucratic mistake. Now she waited, and mentally drummed her fingers. She'd painted the office Cole had allotted her in the building that housed his clinic. She'd overseen the moving in of the new furniture. She'd gone over her files, painstakingly, weeding out, sorting, bringing up to date, but she still had time on her hands and an itch to fill the void.

She should've been happy with her life. Laurie was, and that was a big plus. And Cole insured that Del had everything she needed. Maybe, she thought, she'd feel less edgy if she'd brought more to the marriage than their daughter. Though Laurie was the most important contribution of all, she was not a "worldly possession." Not a stick of furniture was hers. Her secondhand stuff in Florida had been left with the house. Her car had been on its last legs, so it had stayed behind, too, along with all the yard tools, which had been only marginally operative. All she'd brought was the clothes on her back. It gnawed at her that everything around her was Cole's. He'd been unfailingly generous, yet she couldn't rid herself of the unsettling feeling that she didn't really belong at Greenmount.

Greenmount itself was run like a Swiss watch. There were ample personnel for every chore, and everything just ticked along. And with summer in full swing, Laurie left early every morning to attend a day camp with Nat and Judy. They all loved it, and came home dusty, grinning, and exhausted every afternoon.

Cole's business, consisting of the care of myriad flocks and herds, with a big emphasis on horses and dogs, didn't flag in the summer months. With the rabies scare in the surrounding counties, he worked late nearly every night.

But Del was antsy. She needed some activity. She'd

already swum that morning, in the Olympic-sized pool
Cole had had installed in one of the barns. A covered
tunnel led from the house to the barn so that the pool
could be used in the coldest weather New York could
provide. After swimming she'd performed her ritual t'ai
chi, then checked Laurie's, Cole's, and her own clothes
to see if any needed mending. They didn't.

She ambled into the kitchen, where the housekeeper was preparing lunch. "The lawn's getting long. Who
cuts it?"

Mrs. Glyn looked up from her onion-cutting chore,
smacking at her red eyes with the back of her hand.
"Jed. But he won't be coming for a while. Fell off the
thrasher. Lucky he only broke his leg."

"Oh. Lucky. Right." Del looked out the back window at the expanse of lawn. "I guess I could do it.
Mower in the garage?"

Mrs. Glyn looked askance at her, then shrugged.
"The barn where the equipment is kept. Mind the
throttle. It can be a might tetchy."

"Okay." What was the throttle? She'd heard the
term before, but didn't have the foggiest notion what
it was used for. What did it matter? Gas the thing,
start it, and cut. She could remember that much from
cutting her parents' lawn when they'd lived in Geneseo.
It had only been an antique gas mower, with very simple
running instructions. In Florida she'd used an old push
mower for their postage-stamp lawn. "I think I can
handle it. It shouldn't take me long. See you later."

"Fine. Mind the rock garden."

"Oh. I will." Where was that? Front or back? She'd have to familiarize herself with the property more. Rock garden. Her mother had had a small one with "hen and chickens" all over the rocks. Surely the rock garden would be easily visible and she could go around it. She drove a car; steering was not a problem. Buoyed by the feeling that she'd be doing something useful—and time-consuming—that by dinnertime she would've accomplished something, she hurried out the back door.

The July morning was fresh from the rain the night before, but the dew had burned off and the grass would be fine for mowing. The sun would be fierce, though, and she'd read about the possible appearance of Lyme disease in the area. Hurrying back to her bedroom, she redressed in a long-sleeved shirt and thin cotton slacks that she tucked into her socks—prevention against ticks, if the nasty creatures dared to show themselves. Putting a baseball cap on her head, she announced herself ready to tackle the lawn.

Fortified, she headed for the barn again. She assumed Mrs. Glyn had meant the barn nearest the house. She'd seen more than one hand take tack and equipment from there. It was a beautiful, old-fashioned structure, freshly painted barn red like the others on the property, and roofed with black. It fronted on the meadow, where an assortment of four-legged creatures grazed or ran.

As she was approaching the barn, she heard a

honking sound at her back. Looking around, she saw a giant gander, his neck curved in pugilistic warning, coming at her on the run. She could recall how cranky and downright nasty the territorial critters could be, and instinct had her running at a full gallop. She hadn't been out of New York farm country so long that she didn't know how bellicose geese could be, how many farmers used their irascible temperaments to turn them into guard animals.

Sprinting toward the barn, her nearest cover, she threw herself at the door, flung it open, hurled herself inside, then slapped her body against the door to keep it closed. She exhaled in relief as she heard the thumps and angry honking on the other side. Leave it to Cole to have a killer goose on the farm . . . and not tell her about it!

Turning around, she studied the spacious, high-vaulted building. Equipment! And lots of it. Just what she needed. Rakes, spades, hoes, and hay forks of every kind and description hung neatly on the walls. Smaller tools hung above one bench. Above another were instruments that she was sure Cole used in his veterinary work. Unlike most gloomy barns, this one had a skylight jutting out from the gabled roof, letting in the sun. Still, good vision was impeded by the surrounding gloominess.

Del hunted until she found what she needed. "Let there be light," she muttered, turning on the switches next to the door. "Ahh, now I can see. Lawn mower, lawn mower, where are you?"

She didn't recognize it at first, thinking it was a small tractor. But she came back to the green and yellow machine. "Hmmmm, a little large, but they must all act the same." To her relief it seemed to have the same choke system her father's had had, though of course, that one had been on the steering column of the small push mower, not on a panel above the gearshift as it was on the rider.

Del bit her lip, walking in a U around the machine, which had been backed against the wall of the barn. "So there must be reverse," she muttered to herself. Looking it over, she saw the gearshift just below the seat. The other mechanism to one side that looked similar led to the powerful wide blades beneath. "Umm, to lift and lower, I'll bet." She was pleased at her observations, until she noted the lettering that said just that.

Mounting the machine took a little effort, but the springy seat was comfortable. She experimented for several minutes, putting her feet on and off the pedals, testing the steering wheel, operating the clutch and gears. "Pretty simple," she decided.

Taking a deep breath, she leaned down and turned on the key, making sure the choke was in position. When it fired on the first try, blasting the enclosed space with strident, coughing engine sounds, her confidence rose. "I can do this," she said. She put it in first and carefully released the clutch. The mower jumped forward, and she immediately braked. "Easy, girl."

A few minutes later she was steering the machine,

very slowly, toward the door. She braked a few feet from the door, then realized the machine was too wide. Operating carefully, she turned the mower, eyeing the walls. "Ahh, double doors." She drove to the back wall, braked, got off, and managed to slide back the high double doors.

She blinked against the sudden onslaught of sunlight.

A familiar honking had her scrambling back onto the small tractor. Braver with her machine under her, she steered out the door and down the incline to the yard. "Yah, yah, you crabby bird," she shouted to the gander. Though she couldn't hear him over the noise of the tractor, she saw his bill part and his neck curve angrily.

Still moving slowly, she angled around until she came to a large swath of lawn. Stopping, she looked over her shoulder for the gander. It was nowhere in sight. She lowered the blade carefully to its highest level and began to make slow passes across the acre-sized area.

Encouraged by her good fortune, she paused and set the speed up a notch. Better.

Delighted with her mastery of the machine, she stopped three more times, each time raising the speed.

At last she was proceeding at quite a clip, wide swaths of freshly mown grass spreading out behind her in ever-widening waves. Del exhaled, pleased with herself, feeling useful and enjoying the ride on the infernal machine, even if she wasn't totally sure of it yet. She'd definitely be deafened from the constant noise of the engine, she thought to herself.

Deciding to make a cut around the perimeter to ease the turning of the machine without using reverse, she turned sharply and proceeded at the same rate of speed over a knoll that had hidden one side of the yard from her view.

"Oh, glory be. The rock garden!" she shouted. There it sat cuddled into the lee side of the knoll, rock-filled, festooned with perennials, outlined with annuals in pink, green, red, lavender, peach, all the hues in a wild natural setting, beautiful, glorious . . . and coming right at her.

Her feet flew back and forth looking for the brake, her gaze glued to the rough-hewn corner fence that outlined the garden. That would stop her.

She crashed right through it, rocketing over boulders, the blade screeching in protest, the motor roaring. She hung on to the steering wheel, her feet still doing their ineffectual dance to find the brake. "Oh, noooo." She was heading for the driveway, and a truck was coming. It looked like Cole's, but she was bouncing around so much, she couldn't be sure.

The truck stopped as she approached at her rattling, full-throttle roar.

"Del! Dammit, what're you doing?" Cole jumped out of his truck. "Brake! Brake . . . the fence . . ." He ran and vaulted the fence, trying to intercept her. "Stop!"

"Can't," she shouted back. Her feet could find little

purchase on the jouncing, bouncing tractor. Del was sure every tooth in her head was loose. Then she forgot all about that, eyeing the fence that was almost on her. "Oh, dear."

"Get off. Jump." Cole reached out for her and missed.

Del crashed through the white corral fence, wood screeching apart and falling behind her in drunken disarray. "Cole!" she screamed when she saw the donkey in front of her. It neighed and screamed in affronted alarm, then scrambled away, kicking out with its back legs at the noisy intruder.

She felt the jar and sway of the machine as Cole jumped on the blade cover. He found the brake easily. When they stopped, she nearly fell over the steering wheel.

"Lean up, darling," Cole said. "Let me get under you. Quickly. Here comes Feckless."

Del managed to look around him. The donkey was galloping pell-mell right at them. "It looks mad. I shouldn't be here . . . neither should you. Hurry, Cole." She raised up and sat on his lap, her arms circling his neck. "Hurry."

The donkey almost had them, its tobacco-brown teeth snapping before it turned to position its powerful hind legs for the ultimate placekick.

The tractor kicked in, and Cole fired it, running full tilt across the corral.

Del placed her mouth to his ear. "He'll catch us."

Cole smiled, shaking his head. He aimed the tractor right for the opening she'd made and barreled through, then throttled back on the gravel a short distance from his truck. He parked the tractor off the driveway and stopped.

"Hurry," Del said. "Here comes the donkey."

"Don't worry. I don't think he'll leave the corral. He considers it his kingdom." He kissed her forehead. "And he's a mule."

Sure enough, the animal stopped at the opening in the fence, lifting his head and screaming at them, then neighing angrily, all teeth showing.

"Why doesn't he come through?" Del whispered, watching the animal as Cole lifted her to the ground and followed her, his arm going around her waist.

"We're out of his bailiwick; he'll settle for that." Cole looked down at her, lifting her chin with one finger. "How are you?"

All the pent-up excitement, the nerve-wracking ride, and the disappointing end to what should have been such a triumph bubbled up like a caldron of bitter ale. She, who never cried, burst into tears, not even bothering to temper the sound. She howled with anger, disappointment, frustration.

"What? What is it, darling? Del, are you hurt? Where? Show me." His hands ran over her. "Where? Show me, darling."

Del cried louder.

"Del, you must tell me. Where does it hurt?"

"The rock garden!" she gulped.

"What?" He stared at her, then relieved comprehension filled his face. "You're not hurt?"

"No. But the rock garden . . . Ohhh, it's awful."

Amusement overriding his fear, Cole hugged her, kissing the top of her head over and over as he started to chuckle.

"It's . . . not . . . funny," Del said, leaning against him. "I don't know what Mrs. Glyn will say. She warned me about the rock garden."

"She did?" His arm tightened. "What in hell were you trying to do at that speed? Kill yourself."

"Mow the lawn. On the south side it was a perfect speed."

"That area is almost flat, with no dips or curves. The rest of the lawn is another story."

"So I see." She stared at the mule, who stood at the broken fence, still braying. "I don't suppose he has a short memory."

"No. And he's an implacable foe. I've got the teeth marks on my backside to prove it."

"Why keep him?"

Cole shrugged. "No one else wants him."

"Oh." She glanced up at him. He was looking at the irate mule, a smile playing about his mouth. Gentle Cole. Taking a critter no one wanted. "I wonder what Laurie would think of Feckless."

"She's already met him. He likes her." He grimaced when Del laughed. "He still wants to bite me."

Del laughed again, but her mind wasn't on Feckless. She studied the unusual man she'd married. He wasn't a doctor for animals just because it was an excellent way to make a living. He really loved them, cared what happened to them, wanted to help them. And he was no different with humans. He was unfailingly gentle with Laurie, ready and eager to enter into any game with her. And his daughter loved him already. What did she feel as his wife? Certainly pride that he did his work so well. She felt a deeply embedded security with him, too, that she'd never hoped to achieve, that she hadn't even realized existed.

And there was love. It would've been more comfortable for her if she hated him. Love unsettled her, made her feel like she was teetering on a gymnast's balance beam. She didn't want to plumb the depths of her feelings for Cole. She hated the vulnerability, the weakness, the way her knees turned to water and her breathing shortened whenever he appeared. She was no teenager; she'd weathered storms in her life. Yet there were undercurrents between them that she couldn't fathom, that made her nervous, made her want to escape him. Why did he make her feel so threatened? Did he know he was doing it?

Cole led her toward the truck, scrutinizing her several times. "Are you sure you're all right?" She looked rattled, off balance. He was pretty rocky himself. When he'd seen her rocketing over the ground on that damned mower, his heart had stopped. The thought of her being badly hurt, or worse, made his insides turn over. He couldn't lose her again.

"Yes."

Her succinct reply had him scrambling mentally. "I'd like you examined by a doctor."

"You *are* one. And you don't see any bruises," she said lightly.

"I mean it, Del."

"I'm sure I'm fine."

"Then tell me what made you decide to tackle the yard." She was so beautiful, he thought. The fresh air had given her a glow, not the matte tan of the Southern climes, but the old-fashioned rosy glint of Northern sun. Her hair was mussed, but it was still gorgeous as it fell around her face. Her eyes had lost that shuttered, secret look, and were wide, keen, searching. She wasn't fully a woman yet, he realized. No matter what the calendar said, she was an unawakened girl, and she aroused the hell out of him.

As he helped her into his truck, she shrugged and answered him. "I needed something to do. I felt at loose ends."

Cole slid under the wheel and leaned one arm on it, facing her. "Bored?"

Was she? she wondered. Maybe a little disconnected, but not bored. She couldn't believe how happy she'd been to be back in Geneseo. It had been a homecoming, and she relished the good wishes of her old friends and the wonderful bonding with new ones. "No, not bored.

I guess I just wanted to pull my weight." She glanced at him, but his eyes were unreadable. "I hate not being independent. I'm not even as important as the staff—"

"You are to me."

"I'm not used to being an ornament, Cole. I've worked for a living for a long time. And not just because I've needed to, but because I like earning my way. And I want Laurie to feel that way too."

"As do I," he said quietly.

She saw how his face twisted with some strong emotion. "Don't think I'm not grateful—"

"I don't want you to be grateful. What I have is yours, Del, yours and Laurie's. Having the two of you here has given great meaning to my life. Believe that."

"Thank you." She looked down at her hands, feeling like an ingrate. Still, she wasn't totally able to eradicate her feeling of helplessness. What a paradox! Any other woman would have been satisfied being with a man who'd give her everything. And she did appreciate his generosity. But she needed to pull her own weight, and she wasn't sure Cole really understood that. Yet she loved his giving heart, couldn't fault his loving ways. "I . . . I guess I'm being too emotional. Tearing up a rock garden can do that." She tried to smile when she saw his relieved grin.

He put the truck in gear and drove toward the back of the house.

"The mower?" she asked.

"Don't worry. One of the boys will get it." He shot

her a glance. "And don't worry about the rock garden. Ahito will be here next week. He'll tend it."

"Ahito? I thought Lucky and Jed were the gardeners."

"Ahito isn't a gardener. Neither is Lucky. Jed is the main man for the grounds. Mowing is just one of his chores." Cole cleared his throat. "Ahito and I were at Cornell together. He plans gardens for a living."

"Ahito? Ahito Hraga, the famous Japanese landscaper?" Del croaked.

"Yeah."

"Oh, Lord." She turned on the seat to face him. "Don't let him come, Cole. Give me a chance to fix it first."

"Don't be silly. You'll like Ahito, and he's very understanding."

"He'll need to be," she muttered, remembering the devastation below the knoll.

"Want me to take a look at it?"

She shrugged.

Cole drove across the yard and down close to the area. He left the truck and disappeared over the knoll. Del stayed where she was.

In a few minutes he was back, his face expressionless. He slid behind the wheel and put the car in gear.

"Say something," she said hoarsely.

Laughter burst out of him. "I can't wait to see those cutter blades. It took a block and tackle to put some of those babies in there. And you repositioned those

boulders like a giant doing some fancy bowling. Lordy."
His hilarity increased.

"Stop laughing. How much will it cost? I want to
pay for it."

"Don't be silly. Ahito did the garden as a gift."

"Worse," she moaned.

"Relax." He put a hand on her knee. "It's not the
end of the world."

"Not for you."

They reached the house. Cole stopped the truck,
and they got out. "I'm glad I brought Nebbish home
with me when I did," he said. "Otherwise you might be
on your way through town by now."

"I was bound to find the brakes eventually," she
said.

"After knocking down the mayor and wiping out the
trees on the main streets."

"I wouldn't have done that. Who's Nebbish? And
why would you give a creature a name that means 'loser'
in Yiddish?"

"My nurse gave him his name after he ate her
purse." His smile twisted. "Annie said it was the best
she could come up with and not resort to four-letter
words."

"That bad?"

Cole nodded.

"Where is this benighted beast?"

Cole looked around. "Actually, he's usually out of
the truck the minute I stop. He likes to hang around

the kitchen." He grimaced. "Not that Mrs. Glyn like to see him. He's somewhat of a thief."

"A thief?"

"Yes. He steals food, and he's quick." He looked down at Del, seeming to lose his train of thought for a moment. His hand lifted to her cheek, then fell to his side. He glanced away, toward the barn at the back of the house, then at her again. He was frowning slightly. "You can't miss him. He only has three legs. I don't have too many canines like that."

"Oh." Del felt deflated. Cole couldn't seem to concentrate on her. It was as though he wished her elsewhere. "Excuse me, I should go and see if I can do anything with the rock garden."

She was twenty feet from him when Cole snapped out of his unpleasant reverie. He'd been imagining her lost to him, and the thought had made him physically ill. He'd seen enough farm accidents to know what could happen. Too often they were fatal. And another vision had intruded atop the first. Del was bored. She didn't like the farm. She'd wanted more from marriage than she was getting. If she met a man who could offer her what she wanted, would she leave? Would she stay even if she didn't love him?

He berated himself for being stupid. Such musings were for fools. And he wasn't one. At least he hadn't always been. . . .

"Del! Del, wait." He ran after her, catching her upper arm and spinning her around. "Promise me you won't go out on the mower until I've had a chance to show you how to use it."

She sighed. "I'll do my level best not to destroy any—"

"Destroy, be damned. I don't want you hurt. You can use anything on the place. After all, you're part owner, so you'd be using your own equipment. . . ." His voice trailed off at her openmouthed astonishment. "Surely you know you're a wealthy woman now," he said harshly. "And that I intend to take care of you."

"I can take care of myself. I've been doing it for some time."

"I know that," he said tightly. He put his arm around her shoulders. "I'll take you back to the house."

Deflated, she drooped. "I can't. The garden." She and Cole seemed to navigate on parallel lines at times, she mused, especially when it came to discussing her autonomy. Nevertheless, she was determined to be her own person.

"Don't worry about it. It's yours. You can destroy it or keep it."

"I liked what I saw of it," she said, waving a limp hand. "I still can't believe what I've done." She smiled apologetically. "It makes me crazy to think about it."

Her smile made him crazy. What would she say if he pulled her into his arms, threw her down on the grass, and made crazy love to her until they were both smeared with grass stains? He sighed lustily.

"What's wrong?" she asked. "Oh, you're thinking

how much it'll cost to fix the garden. Well, don't worry. I insist on standing for the bill."

Cole studied her upturned face, the lifted chin, the purposeful eyes, the tight lips, and thought her the sexiest woman he'd ever seen. "You must be hell on wheels with the IRS."

Del blinked. "Where did that come from?" she said, then shrugged. "I can kick ass if I have to, but I'd rather use diplomacy. The IRS can play dirty pool at times."

Cole grinned. "I can see how valuable you're going to be to me."

She laughed with him, but she felt uneasy. Was that all she was going to be to him, a business asset? No! She wouldn't be sorry for herself. After all, they hadn't married for love. Their daughter's best interests had been the impetus. Suddenly, the ache in her chest was like an infected tooth, the pain radiating out, making her whole being quiver with the agony of it. Love? A damnable word. And she couldn't love him. She wouldn't let herself. She'd loved him too well the first time. She swung away toward the house.

Cole reached out and caught her hand. "I'll walk you back. I want to make sure there are no adverse aftereffects."

"Feel my nose. No fever. See? I'm just like all the rest of the animals you've cured."

"Except they don't usually have acid in their bark or neigh," he said dryly.

"I don't."

"You do. But more than that, you need a cool shower, iced tea, and your feet elevated."

"Don't you prescribe for me. I'm not a donkey." Raising her head, she stalked away. The heel of one sneaker, which must've gotten damaged on the tractor, came loose and banged crazily against the ground.

"Crazy lady," Cole murmured, and hurried after her.

As they neared the back door, Del asked Cole why he wasn't going straight back to the clinic.

"Why should I?" he answered. "Jamie is good, he likes running the clinic, and Mavis has the rest of the staff in complete control."

"So you're gonna take off the rest of the day, just like that?"

He nodded.

She couldn't stem the smile that lifted her lips. "And what're you planning?"

"Well, I thought maybe you'd like to drive over to the Mount Morris Dam and see the eagles. The last time I was there, there were eleven of them."

"Truly? We never used to have eagles in the area, did we?"

He shook his head. "Since they've started using safer or no pesticides, the habitat and environment have improved radically, and the eagles have returned to New York State. Many of the species were once indigenous to the area."

"I'd like to see that." And she'd love to be with him.

The realization stunned her, but she knew living in a cocoon was no protection. It was just smothering. "I'll need to change."

"I'll go with you."

They entered the kitchen, where Del paused. "Mrs. Glyn, about the rock—"

Cole gripped her upper arm. "My wife loves your rocky road cake, Mrs. G."

"She does? Have I made one since she's been here?"

"Shame on you, Mrs. G. You're getting forgetful." He quickly steered Del out of the room.

"Shame on *you*," she said as they climbed the stairs, "making her think she's forgetful."

"Don't worry, Del. Mrs. Glyn is well aware of her importance around here. Nothing dents her ego on that score."

"You're such a heartthrob."

"That's me." He closed their bedroom door behind them, then turned and hauled her into his arms. "Don't ever endanger yourself again. I haven't got the nerves for it."

He kissed her roughly. When her arms lifted to his waist, he deepened the kiss. Each night they made love, and he held her all night, but every time he kissed her it was as though he were a starving man and she was bread. He never stopped wanting her, needing her, having to touch her. He'd been so intense with her ten years before, and he'd wanted to temper his hot passions after their marriage, but he couldn't hold back.

She filled his thoughts most of the day, and he often dreamed about her at night.

The kiss went on, and Del felt the old familiar pull and heat. Sighing, she let it take her. She'd come to realize that it was useless to fight it. She wanted Cole. She loved having him touch her, and he could take her to the stars anytime he held her and loved her. Nothing was resolved between them. There were glaring inequities in their life . . . but she needed him, she needed him to love her. And she needed to love him.

Cole lifted his head, his breathing erratic. "Maybe we could put off going to the dam for a few minutes."

"How long?" Air rasped from her lungs.

"Long enough for me to love you."

"Did you say a few minutes?"

He grinned lopsidedly. "Maybe a little longer than that."

"I should hope so."

"You sound out of breath. Is that a yes?"

She nodded because she couldn't speak anymore. When he lifted her in his arms, her heart kicked into such a rapid crescendo, she was sure he could hear it.

He went down on the bed with her, his mouth inches from hers. "I like our big bed, because it's fun to chase you around it."

She chuckled. "You don't do that."

"I want to."

"Go ahead," she said daringly, and laughed at his cocky grin.

"I will," he said, and stood, then quickly stripped off his clothes.

Del winced as his shirt hit the floor. "I'll have to sew those buttons back on, and I'm a terrible button sewer."

"Throw out the shirt," he said huskily, kneeling on the bed again. "Run."

Del grinned and started to scoot away from him, arching to slide off the bed.

He caught her before she'd gone five inches. "Gotcha! You can't get away."

"You cheat."

"I always will," he said softly, "if that's what it takes to keep you."

Stopped cold by what he'd said, Del could only stare at him.

"I mean it," he said, then lowered his face between her breasts, letting his lips rove over the soft, smooth surfaces.

Heat spikes drove through her, awakening her afresh to the volcanic desire between them. Marriage was certainly a hotbed of sexiness, she thought hazily as she caressed his head. All those articles she'd read about sexless husbands had to be in error.

Cole lifted his head, his hair mussed, his eyes glazed with passion. "You're beautiful. What are you thinking?"

"I was wondering where all the husbands are that aren't interested in sex. You're not one of them."

"Damn right." He kissed her navel. "And I won't peak until I'm ninety-five. So watch it, baby."

Surprised laughter burst from her. "That long?"

"Longer." His mouth moved lower.

Del saw sparks, reeling stars behind her eyes. Dizzy, giddy, happy, she surrendered to the joy that only Cole could give her. When he stopped caressing her with his mouth, her eyes flew open. He was staring up at her. "What?"

"See, I caught you."

"Yes, you did."

He slid up her body. "Kiss me, wife."

She slanted her mouth over his, kissing him long and hard. When she pulled back, they were both breathless.

"I wanted to be there when you had our child," he said unexpectedly.

She shook her head slowly. "You couldn't have done anything. It wasn't easy." She winced, then added, "It wasn't that bad."

"Tell me."

"We're making love."

"Yes, but first tell me."

Del studied the urgent appeal on his face. Taking a deep, shaky breath, she did. "First babies can be rough, they say."

She paused for so long, Cole almost said something, but her arrested gaze kept him quiet. She'd gone back to that time.

"My parents took me to a lying-in hospital, filled with pregnant women and women who'd just given birth. My mother tried to explain to the nurse that I wasn't married. The nurse just stared at her, then wheeled me away. . . ." She stopped, swallowing hard. "The baby didn't come fast. She was turned around. The labor just went on and on, and the pain was unrelenting. Sometimes I didn't even know I was screaming. They gave me painkillers, but they try to be careful so the child is not affected by any type of drug. But even during the worst of it, I knew my child would be born, and would be fine. They let my mother in at some point, and she told me I had to pay for my sins, even if I died for them. I barely heard her, but I can still recall the stern grief on her face. The nurse hurried her out of the room, my mother protesting every step of the way that I had to know what I'd done, that I had to pay the price . . ."

"Darling, don't. I shouldn't have asked—"

Del shook her head, holding up her hand. "Actually, I'd like to tell you."

"Go on then," he said hoarsely

"Well, I began to get disoriented from the pain. It seemed to come and come. No letup. I thought I was dying. Then, when I didn't think I could do anymore, that I couldn't live . . . she came. I could barely raise my head to look at her. I cried. She was so beautiful, and I loved her right away. . . ."

He pressed his face against her neck, and she heard

a harsh sound, like a sob. Lifting his head, she looked down at the dampness on his face. "Cole?"

"I should've been with you. I could've taken care of you."

Sweet hope rivered through, and she felt passion and peace. "Thank you."

"No. Thank you, Del. For having our child, for making her grow so strong and wonderful, for teaching her how to be her own person, for letting her know that it's all right to be happy and carefree. I'm more grateful than I can say."

Del felt the tears on her own cheeks.

"Now, you're crying," he said, laughing unevenly. He kissed her gently, licking the teardrops from her cheeks. Pressing his body against her, he let her feel how aroused he was.

"Are we starting again?" she asked, smiling.

"Unless you have an objection, ma'am."

"No objections." She closed her eyes, wanting to savor, to treasure every sensation.

"Hey, aren't you going to look at me, beautiful?"

"No, I'm going to enjoy."

He chuckled. "Fine with me. Hang on."

He moved over her like a sexual blanket, his mouth following his hands. He tormented and enticed her, rousing her to heat once more. His tongue slid over her lips, flicking at her cheeks, her chin, her nose. His hands slid down her neck and sides, pausing at her waist to squeeze gently, before fanning over her stomach and lower.

As always there was a moment of pause, when all the reasons she should hold back from this man flooded over her, and she wanted to move away. But he was stronger. Not just his physical hold, but the mental and spiritual hook he had embedded deeply in her with his lovemaking, his care of their child and her. He'd manacled her to him without the least effort.

His touch insisted, took her beyond the hesitancy, as he restlessly sought every pulse point.

Del moaned, not able to stem the joy as her body opened to him.

Feeling her response, Cole pursued her, trying to override all the questions he knew she still had, and giving her back the heat she was giving him.

He knew to the millisecond when she was his totally. At that moment she fired him beyond control, and he had to struggle to hold back. The urge to drive into her again and again was overwhelming. He fought back the passion as his tongue jousted with hers, his hands moving over her neck, breasts, and stomach.

When her body arched toward him, he almost laughed in triumph. Her hands were magic and they roamed him, caressing, fondling, until he thought he'd go out of his mind. "Darling! Don't."

Surfacing out of her euphoria, Del blinked at him. "You like it, though."

"I know, but I can't take it."

She smiled with satisfaction as his head lowered to

her breasts, his lips closing over her distended nipples.

Lost in the silence of desire, she felt his hand move lower, over her belly and lower. In soft sweeps he caressed the triangle of hair between her legs, seeking and finding every hot, damp place until she writhed against him. She wanted to lose herself in him, to be taken and kept by him.

Cole's vague hope of prolonging the ecstasy, of bringing her to fulfillment time after time, faded when she looked up at him.

"Cole," she said pleadingly.

He held his body taut, strain etching his features, as he strove to enter gently. When he was full length inside her heat, he began to tremor as though he'd pull apart. "Don't," he breathed when she pressed up against him.

"Yes," she whispered.

"God!" He opened his eyes and looked down at the mother of his child, the woman who'd given her virginity to him so gladly, the woman who'd raised his daughter and trained herself to be independent, and he knew he was lost. She was here, beneath him, and he wanted to love her, to show her how much she meant to him, how he honored what she'd done and what she was. She was so beautiful, her face flushed, her hair spread upon the pillow. He couldn't forget how she'd been alone, in a hospital where other women had husbands to comfort them, loving families to support

them, and she'd never berated him for not being there.
"Darling."

"What is it?"

"Just darling," he said hoarsely.

"Cole."

At her impassioned voicing of his name he began his climax, feeling her body tremors as she joined him. Again and again he thrust into her. Groans tore from his lips as she lifted her body to meet him. Joined in this wild wanting, they reached for each other, giving, giving in endless love, the spasms bringing them overwhelming joy, excitement, and peace.

He collapsed against her, sated, feeling the flush of passion settle over them like a blanket. He could still feel her tremors, and he wanted to tell her how much he loved her. She had to know.

Instead he cuddled her close and fell asleep with her.

SEVEN

A week later Del still felt as though she was walking a tightrope in her new life. She was sure nothing would be totally resolved until she took the bull by the horns, or, more accurately Cole by the ears. They were dancing around the problem, not meeting it head-on.

Even when they'd gone to the Mount Morris Dam that day and watched the eagles soar over the gorge, they hadn't faced the problems between them. Del knew Cole was bending over backward to please her in every way he could, but he couldn't give her the feeling she needed to have—that she was autonomous, productive, independent. He was too modern, intelligent, and generous a man to want to subvert a woman, but she still had that caged feeling more often than she liked. So much about their life together was good, she argued with herself. Laurie, their lovemaking, good friends. Why couldn't she be satisfied with that? But she couldn't be.

This wasn't the day to deal with it, though, she thought as she applied her makeup. They were entertaining as a family for the first time—and they were having a pig roast!

She rose from her dressing table as Cole walked into the room. "Would it cause an upheaval in the firmament," she asked, "if we decided to have grilled mahimahi with a dill sauce, or braised salmon steaks with herb dressing, or—"

"Del, wait." He took hold of her arms, laughing. "I know you'd prefer fish—"

"It's not that," she wailed. "I just can't bear the thought of killing those animals. No one who comes to this will be that hungry, and yet we're killing all these very nice pigs for their delectation. I hate it." She scowled. "Go ahead, say it. I'm a bleeding-heart liberal, a do-gooder with no sense, or some such thing. Say it."

He pulled her into his arms, kissing her forehead. "I won't, because I happen to be a bleeding-heart liberal and a freaking do-gooder myself. I like being one, and I'm glad you're one."

They did so well when they talked this way, he mused. If only he could plumb the depths of her thinking on other things. Secrets. Del had them. He knew that, and he also had the sinking sensation that he should know what those secrets were. Then again, he felt that in some ways she'd already told him. He'd known she was dwelling on something serious when he entered the room. He wished he could have asked what it was, how he could fix it, but he'd held back. Their connections were still so fragile. He had to hope that time would change that. He'd give the earth to make her happy.

"Look," he said, "Philo Baseheart makes his living at putting on these barbecues. Once he was a steamfitter at Kodak Park, but when times got tough he was one of the ones who had to go. He was out of work for two years until he hit on this as a way to start a business. Would it surprise you to know that most of the people attending feel as you do?"

"Really?"

"Really. It's just that Philo and his brothers are doing better all the time, and I put this on every year as a way of helping out." He pressed a finger to her lips. "Of course, Philo and his brothers, Eli and Henderson, don't know that."

"You're a good man," Del said quietly.

"A good neighbor, maybe." He kissed her, slowly, searchingly. He'd rather have taken her to bed than greet his boisterous friends and neighbors, but the pig roast was always scheduled a year ahead of time, and today was the day. "Don't worry. There'll be salads and dishes like rice and potatoes, and lots of fresh fruit. And if you like, I could sneak off and grill you a nice trout. Digby Horn paid his bill with some really great Rainbows last week, cleaned and frozen. What do you say?"

"No, I guess my appetite for a bit of very crisp pork is rising as we speak. As long as I don't have to look the victim in the eye while they're slicing it." She winced at the thought, but when Cole's arms tightened around her, her brain emptied of everything but the beautiful sensations he could engender in her.

"I promise."

"You're good to me, Cole."

"I want to be. Where's Laurie?"

"At the end of the driveway, waiting for her cousins. Marge promised they'd be the first ones here."

"Shall we go down?"

She nodded, but he indulged himself first and kissed her, long and hard.

Del melted into him. It was all she could do not to beg him to take her, right there, right then. "Better hurry," she squeaked when he released her.

"Gotcha."

As they left the room Del mused over the well-being that had come to her with their marriage. Maybe that was why she hesitated to face Cole about her feelings of helplessness, of not quite belonging because she didn't seem to have a solid place. So much of what they had was rock solid. She hated to risk any of it.

Cole threaded his fingers through hers, and they started down the stairs just as the first car drove up in front of the house. "Here we go."

It struck Del that she liked entertaining with Cole, that she liked being his hostess, his wife, more than anything in the world. It was even more important to her than her career as an accountant!

"Are you all right, Del?" Cole asked, steadying her. "What did you trip over?"

My thoughts. "It was nothing. I just caught my heel."

He tightened his grip. "You have to be careful. If you fell on the stairs you could be badly hurt."

"I'm fine," Del said. They had reached the front foyer, and she stared out the open front door at the woman getting out of the car. "Isn't that Ada Plane, my mother's friend?"

Cole nodded. "I tried to think of people you were fond of and who you might not have seen yet, outside of your classmates." He smiled down at her, then ushered her out onto the front porch.

She glanced up at him, feeling an odd combination of irritation and joy. *Damn you, Cole Whitford, stop giving me reasons to love you.* Then, hearing a woman call Cole's name in dulcet tones, she looked back toward the car. Valerie Tighe had just gotten out of the driver's seat.

"Do you remember Valerie Tighe?" Cole asked her. "She was at our wedding."

"I remember," Del said curtly. *And Valerie Tighe still wants you, Cole. But she can't have you.*

Cole gave her a puzzled look, but said nothing more than, "Shall we greet our guests?"

"Let's," Del said. She had no right to be jealous! she told herself. It was not her business who Cole had been involved with all those years. But now he was a husband, a voice shouted inside her. And Valerie Tighe better know that.

Del watched stonily as Valerie greeted Cole with a kiss on the cheek, and then she smiled and nodded when Cole reintroduced the two of them. That out of the way, Del quickly turned to her mother's old friend. "Mrs. Plane, how are you? It's been such a long time." Del hugged the older woman.

"That's right—you two know each other," Valerie said brightly. "Ada did say she wanted to talk over old times with you. I'll just drag Cole along to the stable and he can show me that mare I'm trying to buy from him."

"I told you, it's not for sale." Cole shrugged at his wife, then followed along after Valerie.

"Tell me how you are, Mrs. Plane," Del said, deliberately turning her back on the couple walking away from them. She led the older woman up the porch steps. "Would you like something cool to drink?"

"No, I'd like to talk to you," Ada said firmly. "And before anyone else comes. I prevailed on Valerie to bring me early for that purpose."

"No doubt it was a struggle," Del murmured though not loud enough for the other woman to hear. She seated herself beside Ada, noting for the first time her agitation. "What is it?"

"I'm going to tell you the truth. They're gone, and the promises I made to them don't count. I haven't that long, you see, and I won't carry it with me."

Del forgot about Cole and Valerie in a very real concern for this woman who'd always been so kind to her. Ada's face had an unhealthy pallor, and she breathed in shallow gasps. "Are you sure—"

"Let me tell you." Ada pressed her hand. She inhaled a deep, shuddering breath. "You're Lena's daughter, Fidelia. I told them to tell you, but they wouldn't. As you know, Alice and Peter lived in Geneseo all their lives, except for one year when Peter worked for the phone company down in Poughkeepsie. That was the year you were born. Lena went to them there, pregnant and alone. When you were born, Lena agreed to let them raise you, though she'd wanted to keep you. You probably don't remember, but she visited you constantly when you were little. Then Alice started worrying that Lena would be a bad influence on you, and she and Peter gave her the money to move someplace else. They were hard on Lena, Alice being ten years older than she, and both her and Peter being so conservative about everything." Ada sighed and leaned back in her chair. "Sometimes I think Alice hated her sister. Lena was so full of life, and she wasn't. When Alice married Peter, they settled into such a dry, lifeless routine."

Del was still trying to take it all in. "Aunt Lena was my mother?" Ada had to be wrong!

"Yes, and your daddy was a fine young man from this area who was killed in a car accident before Lena even knew she was pregnant. They would've married,

I know that. Aaron Wade loved Lena, and she loved him. The Wades were a good family, and he was the best of them." Ada patted Del's knee. "You have one great-aunt left, Fidelia: Phoenicia Wade. She lives on a beautiful horse farm outside of town. She's almost a recluse, now. She knows about you, but she's never told anyone." Ada shook her head. "Was I wrong to tell you? Do you hate me, Fidelia?"

Del slipped onto her knees, hugging the older woman around the waist. "No, no, I'm glad. So often I thought I was a changeling," she said on a sob. "I loved Aunt Lena . . . my mother."

"And she loved you. She wouldn't have left the area to live in California if Alice hadn't insisted." Ada hugged the weeping Del. "They shouldn't have had children. Neither one was fit for the job."

Del looked up at Ada, her eyes swimming. "I tried to love them, and I know they tried to love me. But if only my father hadn't died . . ."

She thought of Cole, and how she'd let a mountain of her own fears outweigh the love between them. Life was too short to do that. She was going to tell him how she felt.

"Are you all right, Fidelia?"

"Yes, yes I am. Thank you, thank you." So many things now made sense. The puzzle pieces fit. Instead of feeling shock or rejection, Del was elated.

*   *   *

Having finally convinced Valerie he wasn't going to sell her the mare she wanted, Cole went looking for Del. He rounded the corner of the house and was about to mount the steps to the front porch when he noticed Ada napping in one of the wicker swings. He paused on the first step.

"Shh, she's asleep," Del said from behind the screen door. "She's not well, and she's alone. I want to help her, Cole."

He nodded slowly. "You sound strange. What's happened?" He crossed the porch and stepped inside, catching the screen door before it could bang shut behind him.

Del wandered into the spacious living room, eyeing the wide-board oak floor and the Indian rugs, made on a nearby reservation, that dotted it. "Do you recall my Aunt Lena?" she asked, not turning to look at him.

"Not well. She left the area when I was a teenager. But I can still remember her smile. It was like yours."

"No wonder. Ada told me she was my mother, and that Aaron Wade was my father."

Cole stared at her in shock. "Your mother? Aaron Wade, Phoenicia Wade's nephew who died almost thirty years ago?" She nodded and he walked over to her, pulling her back against him, his arms crossing over her breasts, his chin resting on her hair. "And how do you feel about that?"

Silence.

"Del?"

"I guess I feel relieved." And she did. She turned in

his arms. "It all fits, Cole. All the recriminations and warnings of dire consequences I heard were tangled up with Aunt Lena . . . I mean, my mother. I don't know how many times they mentioned Lena and what a disastrous life she'd had, but when I'd ask them what she'd done, they'd only shake their heads and say it wasn't fitting." She sighed sadly. "They couldn't have told me, you know. They were so ashamed of Lena . . . and of me, too, I guess. It mattered so much what others might think. I know I was a trial to them. Even as a child I had the feeling they found parenthood a terrible burden."

"They didn't understand your exuberance, your love of life."

She smiled. "Thank you for saying that. There was such misunderstanding all along the line. I knew I failed them, but I also knew they were doing the best they could. They hated that Laurie was born out of wedlock; they strived so hard to keep it hidden." She sighed again. "Now I understand a little of their pain. They must've thought I was cut from the same cloth as my mother, completely immoral to their way of thinking. The thought of having an illegitimate granddaughter *in such a way* must have been so painful for them."

"They didn't know what a winner they had."

She fought back the sobs that were rising in her. "I'm . . . not . . . unhappy . . . I'm not. It's just that I wish I could've known my . . . mother better."

He hugged her close. "I know, I know. I understand."

"I know you do." And that comforted her. Lena would've liked Cole and Laurie. Del slipped her arms around his waist, sighing for what might've been. "I'm going to tell Laurie as soon as possible." And she vowed to herself, I'm going to tell you how I feel, Cole. I've been a fool to hide it from you.

"We'll tell her together," he said.

"Thank you."

"Would you like me to make excuses for you, Del? Today, I mean."

She lifted her head, a shaft of insecurity surging through her. Would he ask Valerie to be hostess? "No, I'm really fine. Actually, I'm happy to know about my mother. It explains so much. And when I tell Laurie about it, she'll be happy too."

"Why not? If I remember right, her grandmother was as beautiful as her mother."

Del was rocked with delight at the compliment. No way would she let Valerie Tighe be hostess at Greenmount that day. Or any day. She was jealous, but she knew that jealousy would dissipate the moment she was finally more open with her husband. "Thank you. I think Lena would've loved you."

"As long as her daughter does," Cole said, and watched the run of blood up her face. "Too soon, Del?"

She shook her head, hesitantly releasing the barriers that had protected her for so long. "Some would say we don't stand a chance."

He stared intently at her. "What do you think?"

She held his gaze. "I think . . . we love our daughter." He waited, but she said no more. "You're hiding a few things from me, wife."

She stepped back. "And don't you hide from me?"

"What would you like to know, Del?"

Do you love me? "Oh, I don't know." She looked toward the door. "I'm sure our guests are waiting." She'd had her chance, and had fudged it again. Stupid.

"Let them wait. There's plenty to eat and drink."

She was tempted to succumb to the temptation he offered. "We can't leave our guests after they've been invited to a—a pig roast."

Cole laughed sourly, disappointment sitting like a rock inside him. He gestured that she precede him and followed her out the door.

On the porch, Del stopped. Why not open up to him now? Would there be a better time? "Cole, wait. I think—"

But before she could say more, someone hailed them, and Cole excused himself. Frustrated, angry at herself, she wheeled around and walked back through the house to the kitchen. Though the barbecue was outside, much of the food that needed refrigerating was in the house. There were refrigerators in the barn, too, to handle the overflow. She could help by taking some of the food out, she decided. And when the damned cookout was done, she was going to talk with her husband.

To her consternation her help was politely declined, so she wandered out back and across the side lawn to eye the long rows of roasting meat, turning slowly on spits. The grills were set a far distance from the tables, on the other side of one of the smaller barns, to keep the smoke away from the guests while they ate. Del knew the tables were already set, so there was nothing she could do there. When she saw some of the attendants carrying trays of carved meat, she hurried across the lawn and offered her services.

A woman with a tall chef's hat looked at her doubtfully. "I suppose you could carry that small roaster over there." She pointed at a tray on which rested a pig's head and several neat rows of sliced crisp pork. "But it's quite a distance to the serving tables on the other side of the barn. . . ."

"I can do it."

"Mind you don't go in the corral. Just follow the others through that barn. It's longer, but you won't tempt some of the vet's animals that he keeps in that corral." The woman shook her head. "Vets are a peculiar lot. Should tie those critters up."

Del stared at the woman, indignant that she should criticize Cole. "That meat tray, did you say?"

"Yep. Be careful."

"Fine, fine, I can do it." Del turned away from the cantankerous chef and walked to the table that held trays of meat. The trays had to be two feet in diameter, and they were hot and loaded.

Taking a deep breath, she hoisted one, wobbled, and steadied.

But when she'd carried the unwieldy tray several yards she began to question if she could manage her burden behind the line that snaked through the barn. Out of breath, staggering a bit, she altered her course. Better to take the shortcut. It would save time, and her arms, already straining, would be relieved of their burden much more quickly. She'd find a lighter job for her next chore.

For now, she had to unload the crisp pork, whose succulent aroma was wafting past her nose. "It does smell good, and I'm getting an appetite for it," she muttered, only half aware of the sound of running behind her. When she did glance over her shoulder, she saw the largest hound she'd ever seen trotting after her. She tried to hurry, even as she thought that a dog, no doubt recuperating from an ailment, couldn't be dangerous. Cole would've told her if there was a dangerous animal in the area.

She increased her speed as much as she could with her heavy burden, causing the meat to slide back and forth on the tray. It had rained the night before and though the day was beautiful, cloudless and warm, the ground was soggy in places between the corral and the barn. She was walking in a particularly soggy area, a wide mud puddle directly in her path. Wobbling precariously, she tried to hurry around the natural barricade. When she heard the growl-bark behind her,

insistent and purposeful, she glanced over her shoulder
again—and lost her balance. Her feet sluiced this way
and that in the soft ground. Mimicking her limbs, the
luscious repast on the platter began the same trembling
dance from edge to edge.

"Go away, doggy, I mean it. Ohhh . . . you nasty
creature. Down. Down, I say! My meat! This is for
the guests, you canine robber. Get away. Get down.
Look out! Damnation and hellfire, the meat—"

Del felt herself lifted by the force of the dog's thrust
to get at the tray. The tray itself became airborne, the
mud turned into a skating rink, and then she felt herself
flying too. "Noooo!"

As if in slow motion, she watched in horror as
the meat scattered in the air, the pig's head spinning
upward like a top. She spun up with it, to come down
with a thud and a brown splash.

The meat and hog's head landed all around her.

For a moment there was silence. Then, from behind
her, she heard slurping.

She swiped at the mud impeding her vision. "Damn
you, dog," she muttered to the happy canine. He was
bigger than a calf, with the jaws of a great white shark.
He crunched contentedly on the head of the roasted
pig, blanketed in sliced pork and pocked with mud.

"Damn you to Canine Hell, dog," she mumbled,
looking down at herself. Her off-white cotton shorts
and matching jacket resembled a brown version of a
dalmatian's coat, though not nearly so neat. Her cot-

ton slip-ons were stuck in the mud. She pushed hanks of dripping brown hair off her brow and tried to dry the drips on her face. "You're a monster." She sat there, gloomily watching the canine with the appetite of a Tyrannosaurus rex devour every scrap of the pig meat and head. "You're going to be very sick," Del said hopefully.

The dog belched mightily, then nuzzled the mud. Finding no more meat, he looked at Del.

"Hey, wait a minute. Did Cole ever tell me about you? No. Then you can't be nasty. So stop looking at me as though I'd just been roasted with an apple in my mouth. Don't start on me, dog. I'm uncooked, and right now, mean enough to bite you back if you try anything."

To her amazement, the huge animal belched again, yawned, then plopped down beside her, putting his muddy head in her lap—and splashing more brown stuff all over her.

"Damn, wouldn't you know. He weighs a ton and he wants me as a pillow. This is just not a good day." Wanting to cry, rage, scream, rail against the twisted Fates that had brought her down, Del leaned back and closed her eyes. Within moments, though, amusement quivered through her. She was the hostess of this hoe-down, and she was up to her ears in mud. She'd give herself five minutes, then get up, roast the dog, and take a shower.

When she opened her eyes, the dog was still there,

and so was the mud puddle. Some of the brown stuff had hardened on her face, congealed on her clothes. "I have to get up, stupid dog. We have a barbecue." Shoving the dog away so she could get up took all her strength. His growl-bark sounded intermittently, though he made no other bellicose gesture.

Rising to her feet, Del started to stretch, but groaned instead. She was stiff and damp and most uncomfortable. "I have guests, lout," she said, scowling at the dog. She had to scrape the crusted mud from her watch.

"No! Good Lord, I've been here for almost—"

"An hour," Cole finished. She glanced up to see him walking toward her. "I've looked all over hell's half acre for you, and I find you in a wallow. Did you misunderstand me, Del? I said we were *roasting* pigs, not bathing with them."

"Very funny," she muttered.

"Are you all right?"

"Shoot that dog," Del demanded, grabbing the dog's scruff and lifting his head. "I'll hold him for you."

Cole froze, noting the canine for the first time. "Del, don't move. Let Restless go."

"Restless, Feckless. You have the oddest names for your odd assortment of animals," she said crossly. "And I won't let him go until you strangle him. He ate my whole tray of pig, head and all. I know you must find that hard to believe, but he—"

"Del! Listen to me. Release the dog and back away.

He can be very unpredictable. He's part wolf, part malamute, and his owners couldn't handle him—"

"I can see why. The animal's an unconscionable thief. I told him not to take the pork. I tried to run." She swiped ineffectually at herself with her free hand. "Look at what you've done, you . . . you lout." She shook his scruff, swaying his head back and forth and bringing him closer to her hipbone.

"Darling! Don't." The animal was more than half wild. And his kind didn't brook nonsense. Cole had known that, yet he hadn't had the heart to put the creature down when his owners had decided he was too unruly. Having a half-wild animal had been all right when he'd lived alone with just the farmhands, before the arrival of Del and Laurie. Now his body pearled with cold sweat as he watched Del with the canine. "Back away," he said softly. "Let me get between—"

"Not on your life. I'm going to tear a strip off this mutt for what he did to me. What are we going to do without my pig?"

"There's plenty more," Cole said, moving slowly to one side, noting how the canine watched him unblinkingly. He paused. "Del, I want you to back away—"

"No, not until I—"

"Del, I'm not asking, I'm telling. That animal is dangerous. He has teeth like razors and twice as big. His paws are lethal enough to tear your face away. Do you understand now?"

"Yes, but—"

"Don't question. This is a very dangerous situation."

Del studied Cole, then the dog. "He's another maverick, isn't he?" At his nod, she put her hand on the dog's head. Though the creature didn't cease watching Cole, he seemed to relax and move closer to her. "He's not like Feckless, Cole. I know," she said quietly. And she knew her husband. He was cut from the same mold. He was a maverick. He'd been born into a warm cocoon of a family where he'd been expected to carry on the tradition of being a lawyer, perhaps even a member of the legislature, as his uncle had been. Instead he'd answered the call of his heart and had reached out to animals, creatures that could never advance him socially or politically. "You show the same compassion and empathy to Laurie and me," she said.

Cole blinked, his concentration slipping off the dog for a moment. "Del," he groaned. "This is no time . . . Not that I don't want to hear what you're saying but— Hey!"

The dog had left Del's side and was ambling over to Cole and looking up at him.

Cole was dumbfounded. When he saw the slight movement of the tail, he was even more taken aback. "This dog had been considered incorrigible, untrainable. What did you put in that pork?"

"My charm," Del said, laughing delightedly, as though the dog's behavior had been her doing. "I think I like the dopey, pork-eating lout . . . though he'll probably get sick from all he's eaten."

Cole shook his head. "He looks pretty good to me." He leaned down, patting the animal. "I guess he wanted to join the party." He glanced at Del. "Let's get you out of here. You have to get in the shower and—"

"Oh, no, I'm not tracking through the house like this. I couldn't stand Mrs. Glyn's long-suffering sighs. I'm sure she hasn't forgiven me for the rock garden yet. Isn't there an outdoor shower I could use? A trough? There must be something."

Cole's frown melted into a reluctant grin. "There is, but it's for the hands. I don't think—"

"I do. Lead the way, and try to find a hidden path. I don't relish looking like I waltzed with the main course in the wallow."

Cole took her hand, then looked around at the sound of a slight growl. "So, old fellow, you've adopted the lady."

"And I've decided to adopt him," Del said. "I like him."

"You should hate him, if half of your tale is true," Cole said. He grimaced when the dog turned and followed them.

Cole led her through one of the dairy barns, out a side door, and into the barn. "Wait here. I'll see if the coast is clear." He didn't like the idea of her showering in the barn, but he was pretty sure he couldn't dissuade her. He looked around and called out. The place was quiet as a tomb. Everyone would be at the pig roast. "Okay, but I'm coming in with you. I don't want anyone wandering into the shower by mistake."

"Then you should remain outside the door . . ." Her voice trailed off as he shook his head. She shrugged, not trying to hide her smile. "Suit yourself." In fact, he was suiting her too: She loved watching him watching her.

The cubicle was small and self-contained, with a white shower curtain as the door. It was quite clean and there were various soaps and shampoos.

Stripping off her sodden brown clothes, she looked at them regretfully and handed them out to Cole. Then she jerked her hand back. "Wait. I have to wear something to the house—"

"Don't worry. There're several bath sheets here, and I'll take you a back way to the house." He pushed aside the curtain and smiled at her, studying her from head to toe. "Muddy but sexy. Very sexy."

"Thank you," she said, grinning. She felt strangely relaxed, and not the least self-conscious. She was growing used to being his wife, to being with him without clothes, as she was every night in the privacy of their bedroom. "Going to shut the curtain?"

"No, I'm going to join you." The sight of her had called to him.

"Are there enough towels?" She wanted him with her.

"Yes. And I wouldn't care if there weren't. I want to be in there with you."

She laughed and backed against the plastic wall. "I don't think this was built for more than one."

"We'll manage." Desire began a hot coil through him. She could arouse him so easily.

"Yes, I think we will." His arms enfolded her. She closed her eyes, sighing with pleasure. "Cole, I want to tell you how I feel about—"

The growl began, grew louder, more menacing. A muzzle with all teeth bared appeared around the flimsy curtain.

"I'll be damned," Cole said softly, more intrigued than intimidated.

"Naughty, naughty. Mustn't do it, Beau," Del said, shaking her finger at him.

The muzzle disappeared. There was a thump, indicating the dog had flopped down in front of the shower.

"Beau?" Cole repeated.

"I thought I'd give him a good name. It's important."

"Now you're an expert." He leaned down and kissed her neck. There was another low growl.

"We might have to put this off until this evening," Del said, trying to shrug within the confines of his tight hold.

Cole glared at the curtain. "Damn fool dog. Get your own girl."

"He's taking care of his mommy. Such a good boy," Del crooned, making Beau's tail thud hard against the floor. Del laughed.

"Lord," Cole moaned. He snapped the curtain tightly shut and turned on the water. Taking the shampoo, he washed her head. "I can't believe I'm doing this and not making love to you. I could pass out from the strain." He kissed her nipples. "I love your body."

"And I love yours," Del said. "But we have to hurry."

"Are we ever going to have enough time alone?"

"Probably not." She kissed his chin, vowing to make the time to bare her soul to her husband.

Finally, wrapped in bath sheets, they cautiously exited the barn, with Beau at their heels.

"What did you do with my clothes?" Del asked.

"Threw them out."

"Cole! That outfit was expensive."

"And beyond reclaiming. I'll buy you another outfit. Ten outfits." He looked around and pulled her hand. "Let's go. We'll go in the front door."

"What? Everyone will see us."

"No they won't. They'll be eating out back. No one will be in front of the house. Damn dog still with us?"

"Yes, he is. I like him."

"I should've known you'd be the one to tame him."

"Why is that?"

"You do the damnedest things."

Del's heart jolted in her. Was Cole pleased? More than likely he was damn sick and tired of having a wife who didn't pull her weight, who hadn't begun to earn anything, and who damaged the grounds and the food. Not a good record.

They made it to the front door without incident. It was as they were going up the stairs to the second floor that they heard voices.

"I can sic the dog on them," Cole muttered.

"No, bring him upstairs with us."

"What?"

"Well, he might scare someone if we left him down here. You said he was considered incorrigible. Someone might not understand that he's gruff, but has a heart of gold."

"Right," Cole said dryly.

Del had to laugh. "You can see I'm right."

"It's crazy—but then, our whole life is." He whistled to the dog, not noticing how the smile fell off her face.

He was joking, she thought. Right? Was he happy with Laurie? Yes. With her?

On that one, she decided to take the fifth. "Let's go," she said.

The three of them made it to the master suite, the dog making strange sounds in his throat.

"He's happy," Del said.

"It might be colic."

"You know it isn't."

"I guess you've adopted him."

"Unless you won't let me."

Cole shook his head. "He's yours. Just let me check

him now and then. He had a bad reputation." He eyed the dog. "But truthfully I've had the feeling it was mostly bad handling."

"There you are."

"I still want to keep an eye on him."

"He's just been maligned," Del said, tossing off her towel.

Cole stared.

She noticed and reddened with delight and shy happiness.

"I hope you know what you're doing to me," Cole said hoarsely. He pulled his own towel off and advanced on her. "To hell with the guests and the dog."

Del backed away regretfully. "We can't, Cole. We have to put it off until later . . . but I will admit . . . I've got the hots for you, too, doctor." She would've laughed when Cole groaned, but she herself was feeling such an ache of sexual want, she couldn't manage.

For the first time in many years she felt carefree, unfettered, unconditionally happy. And she couldn't pretend it was anything or anyone but Cole who'd wrought the change. She'd found out she had a mother, a laughing, beautiful individual who'd thought it was fine to enjoy life and to taste the fruits of happiness, and who'd sacrificed her right to live in her own hometown, instead banishing herself across the continent in order to ensure what she thought would be a stable upbringing for her daughter. If Del hadn't come back with Cole, she might never have known about her mother, never understood the monumental giving that love is, never seen her daughter's joy in having a father.

Cole suddenly took hold of her upper arms. "Tell me."

"What?"

"About what you're so happy about."

"Oh. Well, what Ada told me, seeing Laurie so happy, and a lot more."

"For a lady who just discovered her true parentage, you're acting pretty casual. Tell me the secret." Cole slid his hands down to grasp hers. He couldn't bring himself to release her. They'd crossed some battlefields together that afternoon, and they were neither wounded nor shell-shocked, and he needed to know why.

"I fully intend to, Cole," she told him solemnly. "I've just discovered the only way to be free is to untie yourself from absurdities and uncertainties."

"Where the hell did that come from?"

"You." She smiled saucily, then hurried to the dressing room to don her clothes.

"Del! Tell me what you're talking about."

"I will. Get dressed. We're having a party." Within minutes they were almost ready.

Cole, as he was wont to do, watched in the mirror while she did her hair and makeup. "I like watching you do this."

"Feel free to drop by anytime."

"I will." He kissed the top of her head.

Nearly euphoric, they left the house, circling around

it to the backyard. The sounds of laughter and conversation grew louder.

"You still haven't told me what made you so happy today," Cole said, swinging their hands between them. "You're different."

"A decision."

"Which is?"

Del greeted some people, then turned to him. "I've decided to bait the tiger rather than try to stroke the kitten."

Cole stopped walking. "Cryptic as hell, aren't you? I assume you're saying that you're not going to be a bridge over troubled waters, but rather a whip, gun, and chair advocate."

Del's heart palpitated with amusement and sexual heat. That was the crazy thing about Cole. He could drive her wild with desire and make her laugh at the same time. "Yes. I've decided to beard the lion in his den."

"And mix your metaphors into a soup."

She waved her arm. "Picky, picky. Let's rejoin our guests."

Much to her surprise, Del did enjoy the crisp skinned meat of the pig, and she found the vegetables and salads delicious.

Wherever she went, Cole was at her one side, Beau at the other. She had no worries about the dog until Laurie came running pell-mell toward her parents, red-faced and laughing. When Cole heard the dog growl he quickly placed himself between his daughter and the canine.

"What's the matter with the dog?" Laurie asked. "Is he jealous?" She grinned when her parents looked surprised and nodded. "I guess we'll just have to get used to each other." She held her hand out to the dog.

"He might not understand," Del said. "Your father says he's half wild."

Cole's blood dropped to his shoes when Laurie knelt in front of the animal, crooning to it. Everything he'd ever heard of what a wolf could do to another animal ran through his mind. Panic had him reaching out for his daughter, but his wife stayed him, putting all her weight on his arm.

"Don't!" she whispered. "Laurie has your magic with animals. Watch."

Stunned, Cole did, though his body trembled in readiness. He wouldn't let anything harm Laurie.

When his daughter laughed, trying to avoid Beau's lapping tongue, he relaxed. She hugged the animal, and he went down on his haunches, edging closer.

The oversized beast turned, almost casually, throwing its hip at Laurie, keeping the girl behind him. Eyeing Cole, he growled a low warning.

"Even I can see she's safe," Del said, putting her hand on his shoulder.

Cole nodded. He pulled her hand around to his mouth and pressed his lips to her palm, his tongue touching there for a moment.

Lightning flashed through him, enclosing him in the wonderful aura of both family and sexuality. He'd never felt so secure, even though he felt a lacing of fear as he studied the calf-sized dog in front of him. Then Beau touched his knee with its nose, and he crossed the chasm of wariness between man and beast.

"Okay, big fella, I understand. I've made the same choice about her." Cole grinned at his daughter when she laughed, but the feeling of his wife's hand caressing his neck sent desire cascading through him. He reeled with the wonder of being parent and lover, and he could've shouted his joy to the sky.

"I want to show him to my cousins," Laurie said. "Don't worry, I'll explain to . . ."

"Beau," Del said softly, chuckling. "See that you keep him in check. I don't want anyone frightened by him."

Laurie frowned at her mother. "He won't do anything wrong. He's a sweetie face, Mom. You know that."

Her parents watched her stroll away, the dog, who came almost to her shoulder, trotting happily at her side.

Cole winced when he heard a modified shriek. "Some of our guests won't be thrilled."

"Then let Laurie tell them. She's quite articulate at times."

He shook his head, grinning. "She's so much like you. Feisty, cocky, never-say-die."

Del looked up at him, amazed. "I don't think you would've said that if you could've seen me struggling after my parents died."

"Oh yes, I would, because I would've seen you struggle to get an education, take care of a baby, and get a job so that you could raise the child the best way possible. I admire you a great deal, Del."

"Thank you." She glanced up at him. "I guess it was no small feat to fly in the face of tradition and become a vet instead of a legal eagle."

He smiled crookedly. "I'd had every intention of informing my father, as I later did my uncles, that I truly didn't enjoy practicing law, but he died."

She saw the flash of pain in his eyes, and loved him for the deep emotion he felt for his family. She envied him that. "I would've loved to have been able to tell my mother I loved her."

Cole studied her, then kissed her forehead. "I think she knows." He looked over his shoulder. "C'mon, wife, I'm going to feed you again. There's too much food and we shouldn't waste it."

She stared at the mounds of meat and half-filled bowls of side dishes. "Pack it up and send it to the local soup kitchen. It could feed an army. As for myself, I couldn't look at another boar's head with vacant eyes."

Cole laughed. "Your wish is my command."

Later that night, after they'd tucked Laurie into bed, with Beau lying on the floor beside her, Del and

Cole readied themselves for bed. Cole waited until Del had climbed in beside him before speaking.

"Will you tell me now, Del, what all your cryptic comments today mean?"

She smoothed her satiny nightgown down her legs. "To begin, I've been all at sea because I don't have my license yet, so I can't work."

"I know."

She put her hand under her chin, staring at him. "Everything here is yours—"

"And yours."

"You've been most generous. But I need to pull my weight, do something."

"Hence the lawn mower incident and the spilled pork."

"Yes." She smiled at him. "But I realized today that it's been my insecurities, not your ownership of Greenmount, that's been the problem. I wasn't able to value myself as just myself and as—as your wife. I thought I was failing you because I wasn't a productive, money-earning member of the household."

He pulled her close to him. "I've always valued you—who you are, what you can achieve." His arms tightened around her. "I don't want anything to come between us."

"It won't. I won't let it anymore. I know I can be my own person, no matter what I do." She eased back to touch his cheek. "I feel stupid that it's taken me so long to realize it."

He kissed her gently. "I love you, Del. And I'm so damned proud of you."

"I love you too."

That night their lovemaking took on a special feeling, a cascade of giving passion that rocked both of them.

EIGHT

"I've never been to a State Fair. I mean it, Cole."

Cole took his gaze off the thruway momentarily, looking at her in disbelief. "That can't be." He glanced in his wide side mirrors and signaled to pull out in the passing lane, his hands sure on the buslike steering wheel of the huge RV. "You were in dressage when you were young," he said.

"Only for about a year." She smiled at him. "How can you remember that? I've never thought much about it."

"I remember seeing you at one of the competitions. You were nervous, but determined."

She laughed. "That was me." Her smile faded. "Maybe I blocked it from my mind because I really wanted to do it, but I was only able to go to local competitions. My parents didn't think it was worth the money to go out of the area. And if it hadn't been for a neighbor supplying a horse, I wouldn't even have competed locally." She shrugged, feeling no animosity toward the man and woman who'd raised her. "They were very conservative and considered such things extravagant."

"I saw my cousins' RV behind us, Dad," Laurie said, coming from the back of the well-appointed vehicle. "I like our bathroom." She stretched up to kiss him on the neck before returning to her seat.

"Buckle up," Cole said, glancing over his shoulder at her.

"I did." Laurie grinned at him, then curled up with her arms around Beau, who now accompanied her everywhere. "I wonder if I'll be able to take Beau to school with me. He'd miss me so much if I was gone all day."

"He'll have to get used to it," her father said.

"I suppose." Laurie sighed, hugging her dog and closing her eyes.

Del looked over her shoulder in a few minutes and saw that both of them were asleep. Looking in her side mirrors, she noted the smaller but still roomy rig behind them. "It was good of you to give that RV to Marge and Sid."

Cole shrugged. "I was glad to do it. Sid's was given to me by a very grateful owner of one of my patients. We didn't need two, and I knew we'd all be happy if Marge and her family came along."

"Thank you." You could've sold the other RV and made a profit, Del told him silently. Instead you gave it to our friends, and even offered to store it in our barns when it isn't in use. He was an amazing man, and she couldn't believe how happy she was being married to him. Every day, it seemed, he did more for people, or for her and Laurie, always taking that extra step, shying away from praise or gratitude, just grinning in that lopsided way of his, like it was nothing. More and more she was enthralled by him and frightened by the depths of her love for the man she'd married. Frightened because she was quite sure she'd be devastated if she ever lost him.

"What're you thinking?" he asked.

"About the State Fair," she said, then groaned inwardly at the deception. "No, that's a lie. I was thinking how good you are, and how happy I am to be your wife."

He sent her a torrid look. "Will you tell me that tonight when we're in bed?" he asked huskily.

"Yes." She reached over and tapped his thigh, feeling powerful, content. "I'm looking forward to seeing the Fair."

"So am I." He caught her hand and kissed it quickly.

The rest of the journey to the fairgrounds in Syracuse was pocked with long silences and casual conversation. But the air vibrated with emotion, the anticipation of greater togetherness.

* * *

The fairgrounds were bursting with activity, with people running hither and yon. Cole carefully drove to the RV parking area, maneuvering the large vehicle into the space. He shut off the engine and turned to Del.

"I should go right to the stables. I need to check Valerie's horse for—"

"Valerie's horse?" Del interrupted, shifting to face him.

"She competes in dressage," he said. "Didn't I tell you that? She's quite a horsewoman."

"I'm sure," Del muttered. She pushed open her door and stepped out of the RV.

"Del, listen—"

"Daddy, let me out. I want to see Judy and Nathan," Laurie called. "And Beau needs a comfort walk."

Cole looked at Del, grinning. "Interruptions. That's our life." He got up and walked into the back of the RV. "All right, honey. Take your pooper scooper with you. You know the rules."

"Yes, yes, you told me a million times." Laurie left with her dog in tow, waving to the two children exiting the other vehicle. "Hey, you guys, isn't it neat?"

Del watched Marge approach, smiling when her friend looked at her cross-eyed. "Too much for you?" Del asked.

"Actually, having the RV was wonderful. They ate, they fought, they slept, they fought, but I could be pretty much removed from it because they had things to do. I really like those vehicles." She looked around. "I can't believe I've only been to this Fair once, and you've never been. We have to get out more, friend. Sid and I thought we'd take the kids to the midway. You and Cole want to tag along?"

"I'll go, but Cole has to check on some of the cattle and horses over in the barn."

"Whoops, do I hear a little acid in thy tone, friend?"

"No," Del said sharply, then looked apologetically at her friend. "I'll be a minute. I need to tell Cole where I'll be." At Marge's nod, she entered the big RV. Cole was just coming out of the bedroom, his medical bag in his hand.

"Want to join me in the barns?" he asked.

"I'm going with Marge and Sid . . . taking the kids to the midway," she said, wishing she hadn't made plans so impetuously.

They stared at each other, then he leaned over to kiss her cheek.

"Okay, Del, I'll see you later."

She thought she saw a hurt look in his eyes. "Cole, I—"

"I should go. I promised I'd be there forty-five minutes ago."

Del moved aside. As he passed she held her breath, hoping he'd kiss her again, but he went by and exited the vehicle.

* * *

"Go, for heaven's sake," Marge said.

"What?" Del looked up at her friends as she sat on a bench waiting for one of the rides to end. Laurie, Nat, and Judy were on it. Sid and Marge stood above her, sipping sodas and watching her with exasperated amusement.

"You'll walk into a wall if you don't join Cole," Marge said. "You've had him on your mind since we came out on the midway. Now, get out of here. We're going to take the kids for a soda and a hot dog after the next ride. They'll be thirsty and hungry. You find Cole."

Del wasn't going to argue. She wanted to be with Cole. They were right. Smiling weakly at her friends she rose waving to the children as they went by in their bumper car. They laughed and waved back, then were gone again.

"I'm outta here," she muttered, then she was sprinting down the midway, making a right turn through some stands, then a left past a group of eateries until she spotted one of the stock barns.

Taking a chance on the first one, she headed into the gloom of the high-domed building. Brahma bulls, cows, cattle of all sorts. No tall, handsome vet.

She tried the next barn. Sheep, goats. The next one held pigs. Startled at the size of some of them, she had to stare. They had the bulk and breadth of steer.

She tried the next barn. Horses!

Moving slowly in the gloom, she searched for Cole.

"Well, well. Have you come to try your luck at dressage?"

Del turned slowly. "Hello, Valerie."

"Hello, yourself. Cole isn't here." The other woman's arch smile seemed a fitting accessory to the elegant riding togs of a dressage competitor.

"Really?" Del said evenly, swallowing her animosity. "Then I'll go over to another barn and look for him."

"Why don't you do that?" Valerie said. "It's downright diverting to watch you run after your husband in such a Victorian fashion."

Del was smoking. "How clever of you to notice. And how would you describe the method *you're* using to chase my husband?" She spun on her heel as the other woman gasped.

Blindly, Del headed up one aisle of horses and down the other, seeking an exit, an escape from the hurt. That woman! She wanted her husband. Well, dammit to hell, she wasn't going to get him. She'd had ten years to nail him and she hadn't. And now he was Del's. That monumental truth hit her just as a huge Clydesdale was led down the aisle toward her. "Good Lord," she whispered, as the animal, at least seventeen hands high, stopped in front of her. When he snorted and bobbed his head up and down, she had the greatest urge to run. Still, as his handler tried to grab the horse's snout, Del stayed his hand. "Don't. I think he wants to say hello."

"Generally, ma'am, these animals is as gentle as you can get. Angus isn't one of those. He's mighty particular about his friends," the man said, huffing slightly.

Del patted the wide, long nose, and when the animal quieted she smiled.

"Well, I'll be," the handler said. "You must be one a' his choices, ma'am."

"That's because you don't know my wife's way with animals," Cole said at her back.

Del spun around, almost smacking the horse's nose with her head. "Cole! I didn't think you were here. . . ." Her voice trailed off at his puzzled smile. "I mean . . . I thought . . . someone said you were elsewhere," she finished lamely.

He shook his head, his smile lopsided. "I take it you weren't looking for me."

"No, I was looking for you. I wanted to watch you work," she told him truthfully. Pleasure washed his face in a smile, and she felt delight that she could make him happy. "May I?"

"I'll put you to work," he said. He leaned down and kissed her on the mouth. When Angus's handler snorted, he lifted his head. "Nothing better than to kiss a beautiful woman, Eldred."

"I can see that," Eldred said.

Cole took her arm and led her into the stall beside them. "Angus needs a shot. He lost his footing and caromed into barbed wire. Infected. He's almost well, but needs another shot of antibiotic."

"I'll hold his head."

"You canna, ma'am," Eldred said. "This fella is strong and the minute he's touched back there, he'll rear. That's why I'm here."

"Then I'll talk to him," she said. "Be careful, Cole. He's awfully big." She glanced worriedly at hooves the size of platters, then walked over to the horse's head. "Beautiful boy," she crooned, patting the creature, muttering inane love words to it. The horse was as still as a statue.

"Done," Cole said. "I'm going to hire you. What do you think now, Eldred?"

"I think your wife's a flaming magician, that's what I think," Eldred said. He eased and shoved the Clydesdale back into his stall and closed the Dutch door that would allow the giant equine to look out.

When the creature nickered at Del, Cole laughed with his wife, putting his arm around her. "I'm glad you came."

"Cheap help?"

"Well, there's that." He laughed again when she slapped his arm. "I wanted you to see me work," he added abruptly.

She stared at him, her hand going out to him. "You're very impressive . . . and I think you should take Laurie along on some of your calls. I would like her to understand what her father does." At the surprised pleasure on his face, she felt a rush of guilt. Was she so insensitive to his needs that she'd not surmised how he'd feel about having his daughter by his side, watching him work?

"Shall I tell you something else, Dr. Whitford?"

"Be my guest."

"I'm here for a number of reasons. Because I love you, because I'm proud of you, because I want to watch you work . . . and because I'm so damned jealous of Valerie Tighe, that if she bats her eyes at you again, I'll punch her lights out."

Eldred guffawed and ambled into the next stall.

Wide-eyed, Cole gaped at her. "But why be jealous? There's no one but you. And you know I love you."

"Yes. But I still am." She clenched her fists. "And I'm still going to get her if she goes after you again."

Cole struggled against the laughter, but it wouldn't be contained. He roared, then pulled Del into his arms, kissing her long and hard. "I do love you, Mrs. Whitford." He grinned. "Only because you're a first-rate accountant, though."

"Rat," she told him inelegantly, then threw her arms around his neck and kissed him. "I'm proud to be your wife, of what you do, and of what you've done." She stepped back. "Now, where do we go?"

"This way." Cole pulled her close to his side and they started down the aisle.

"Yessir," Eldred muttered, currying the Clydesdale with long, sure strokes, "that's what she is—a magician."

"I like you this way," Cole whispered to Del as they walked along. "There will always be new levels of you to know. I like that."

She touched the corner of his mouth with one fingertip. "More importantly, I'm beginning to understand myself."

They continued on, until Del stopped suddenly, nearly tripping up Cole. She turned to him, her expression thoughtful. "I rather like Angus, but I don't think Eldred does."

"Not many people do like Angus. He's had a checkered career, and some pretty rough handling."

"Maybe we should take him."

"Too late."

"Someone's got him," she said, crestfallen.

"Yes. I told the Mentors, his owners, that I'd arrange something else for him instead of putting him down as they suggested. You see, they bought him to show, because he might be the biggest Clydesdale in the area, maybe the country. But because his nature has become pretty rough, totally unlike the breed, they now want to get rid of him."

"Well, I hope his new owners will try to understand him."

"They will. . . . It's you, Laurie, and me."

"Oh, Cole." She threw herself into his arms, hugging him tightly.

He yanked her to him, lifting her off her feet. "Del!"

A moment in time held them. Loath to break the

spell that had engulfed them, they held each other, oblivious to the neighs and whinnies.

At last Cole pulled back. "Let's go back to the RV and—"

"Cole!" A woman's voice called out. "There you are. I need you to look at Wildwind. I'm worried about her fetlock again." They both turned to see Valerie sauntering toward them. "Oh, Del, I see you hunted your husband down. Cole, you wouldn't believe what a bloodhound your wife is. She was hunting for you everywhere."

"Get Archie, Val," Cole said, referring to the other volunteer vet. "Del and I are going to kick back for a few minutes and—"

"Oh, I can't. I'm first out of the gate this afternoon. You have to do it."

"Do it, Cole. I'll help." Del grinned at Val's open-mouthed surprise. "I'm a whiz with animals, two- and four-legged," she said blithely. "Lead the way, Val, old girl."

"Stall thirty-six," the other woman said tightly.

Cole winked at Del, his eyes knowing and amused.

It didn't take long to check Valerie's mount. Then, because Del discovered that some of the other entries were also patients of Cole's, she insisted they sit in the stands and watch the indoor event.

"I'd rather be back in our king-sized bed in the RV," Cole muttered, frowning at his wife when she laughed.

"How many of these horses are your patients, Cole?"

"Four of them."

"It's a very graceful and skillful exercise, isn't it? I can recall how much I liked it."

"Yes. I thought, if you agreed, we'd get Laurie started—in a small way, of course."

Del nodded. "I think she'd like that. She loves all animals."

The conversation went back and forth between them, but their innocuous words were like red-hot coals between them, each one more torrid and loaded with meaning than the last. When the competition was finally over, there was open hunger in their glances.

"Let's leave," Cole said abruptly.

But their exit from the dressage area was impeded by the many who stopped to speak to Cole or ask his advice.

Finally they were walking back to the RV. They'd be alone!

Just as they reached the vehicle, the door was flung open and Laurie all but fell out, with Beau and her cousins at her heels.

"Hi, Mom, Dad, we're watching television. Aunt Marge and Uncle Sid are napping in their RV, so we decided this would be the best place for us. Can we make popcorn?"

"*May* we make popcorn," Del said absently, feeling gray and disappointed, and ready to kill her best friend.

"Huh? Oh yeah, good English. I remember. Can we?"

"Yes," Del said, glancing at Cole, who grimaced as his daughter hopped back into the vehicle. "Isn't parenthood fun?"

"Great. When do we get to be alone?"

"On a trip to Istanbul?"

"I'll arrange it in the morning."

The rest of the stay at the State Fair was filled with fun. At Laurie's pleading, Del even tried the Ferris wheel, though she kept her face in Cole's shoulder the whole time.

On the drive home, Laurie slept, with Beau at her side.

"She was ecstatic when you told her about Angus," Del said, watching the passing landscape lazily, more contented with life than she'd ever been.

"He should manage to break us in a few short months. They have great appetites."

"I'll get a job."

"You *have* a job. Maybe I'll camp on your doorstep."

"I'll keep the door unlocked."

His quick glance was met by her dazzling smile. When he groaned in frustration, her smile widened.

"I think I'll try to buy one of those old Chevies with the big backseat." As soon as the words were out, Cole wished them back. Those had been tough times for her. She didn't need any reminders. "Del, listen, I'm . . ."

At her shout of laughter, relief and pride flowed through him. She'd faced her bête noire and conquered it. He grinned at her. "Have I ever told you that I think you're special."

"No," she said, still chuckling, "but feel free to extol my virtues anytime."

"I can, and will," he whispered, "tonight in bed, where I can hold you and kiss you and make you hot."

It was Del's turn to groan.

That evening, when Laurie was in bed, Del and Cole took a long, hot shower together.

"You're beautiful, Fidelia."

His look made her believe it.

"There's so much I want to tell you, Del, but all I can do is look at you." His hands roved over her slick-wet skin, pressing, probing. She returned the favor, running her hands over him.

"You made me so happy today," he went on. "Oh, not because you told me you were jealous of Valerie, but because you finally told me what was hurting you. I needed to know that, love."

She shook her head. "I was stupid. I should've told you right away."

He nodded, hesitating. "Del, I should tell you something." He took hold of her bare shoulders, rivulets of warm water giving them a sheen. "I've been jealous too." He exhaled. "I'm glad that's off my—what is it? You look shocked."

"I—I am. Cole, I thought I was the only one."

He grimaced. "No. I'm not proud of how possessive I felt when we first met again, how I wanted you near me all the time, how I bristled when you talked to other men . . . even Sid." He winced when she chuckled. "I'm a jerk."

"No you're not." She rubbed her hands over his wet face. "We were insecure with each other. Falling in love at a young age is a handicap. Neither one of us believed our love would last."

He shrugged. "Maybe. But when I saw you at the reunion, I knew you were for me. I loved you years ago. I love you now. Aww, baby, don't cry."

"Then don't say such nice things." He turned off the water. They dried each other, then he lifted her into his arms. "I want you, Del, for a lot of reasons, but primarily because life without you would be nothing."

"Me too."

He placed her on the bed and lay down beside her, warmed by the passion glinting in her eyes. "Sometimes I can't believe I'm yours."

"Believe, Whitford, because I'm yours."

"Yes," he breathed against her neck. His mouth moved down her body, pausing to suckle her breasts, his libido climbing when she moaned.

Their lovemaking had a special vibrancy, an urgency that melded them together in the fiery passion that had been theirs since they were young. Rather than waning, it had waxed hotter with time, gaining more depth and breadth of feeling than either had ever imagined possible.

For long minutes afterwards, Cole simply held her. Then he whispered in her ear, "Was it good for you?" He laughed when she punched his arm, then swallowed her mirth in a long tender kiss.

"I love you, Del."

"Me too."

Later, cuddled to his side, Del listened to his light snoring and smiled. If she could hear that sound all her life, she'd be content. She frowned for a moment. Maybe she should tell him what she suspected—that he might be a father again come Valentine's Day. She still couldn't deal with the elation she felt. Somehow it had seemed that she would never have another child. Now she would. Happiness sizzled through her as her eyes drooped shut and she snuggled closer to her man. Time enough to tell him in the morning.

EPILOGUE

Thanksgiving Day

"Why did you have to invite so many people to dinner today? You're in a delicate condition." Cole's eyebrows snapped together when his wife laughed. "Well, you are."

Del shook her head. "I'm pregnant, not sick. I didn't have morning sickness or any of the other side effects. Dr. McBride says I'm healthy as a . . . horse." She laughed harder when Cole glowered at her humor. "What's to worry? You're a doctor and—"

"A veterinarian! Dammit, Del, you have to take care of yourself."

"I do." She went to him, laying a tender hand on his cheek. "You should be calm, doctor. Instead you're amusing."

"I don't think it's funny. You'll tire yourself with that crowd coming today."

She shook her head. "Mrs. Glyn is doing most of it. The hands on the farm have helped, too, and Marge is doing a great deal." She paused. "And Great-Aunt Phoenicia is bringing cookies."

"And Ada, and a few more people from Seaforth," Cole said, referring to the estate of town houses and condos for the elderly where they'd placed Del's aging relative. She loved it and was doing well, delighted that Cole had taken over her horse farm and was managing it. "I want the people here, Del, you know that. I just don't want you tired out."

"I won't be."

He took her in his arms, trying to mask his anxiety. She was in good health; her doctor was pleased. He had to keep telling himself that. "You're happy about becoming so close to Phoenicia, aren't you?"

"Very. Laurie loves her too."

"Yeah." He put his chin on her head. "It's been a great year, the best of my life, thanks to you . . . and a class reunion."

"It seems like it couldn't all have happened in such a short time, yet it has." She glanced up at him. "Next spring there'll be another reunion. Shall we go?"

"By all means. I can't wait to see what will happen to us next year, Mrs. Whitford."

"I'm so happy, Cole. Today I'll have so much to be thankful for, and next year at the reunion, I'm going to get down on my knees and thank the Almighty for sending me you."

"I love you, Del."

"Me too."

On Valentine's Day the local vet almost fainted at the birth of his son. The nurses stopped laughing when they saw the tender way he hugged and kissed his wife.

"I wish I could meet a man like that," one said to the other.

"Don't we all," the other nurse sighed.

The vet didn't hear. He was too busy hugging his wife and telling her how much he loved her.

THE EDITOR'S CORNER

July belongs to ONLY DADDY—and six magnificent heroes who discover romance, family style! Whether he's a confirmed bachelor or a single father, a small-town farmer or a big-city cop, each of these men can't resist the pitter-patter of little feet. And when he falls under the spell of that special woman's charms, he'll stop at nothing to claim her as a partner in parenting and passion. . . .

Leading the terrific line-up for July is Linda Cajio with **ME AND MRS. JONES**, LOVESWEPT #624. Actually, it should be *ex*-Mrs. Jones since high school sweethearts Kate Perry and Mitch Jones have been divorced for eleven years, after an elopement and a disastrous brief marriage. Now Kate is back in town, and Mitch, who's always been able to talk her into just about anything, persuades her to adopt a wise-eyed injured tomcat, with the promise that he'd be making plenty of house calls! Not sure she can play stepmother to his daughter Chelsea, Kate tells herself to run from the man who so easily ignites her desire, but she still remembers his hands on her body and can't send him away. To Mitch, no memory can ever match the heat of their passion, and he's been waiting all this time to reclaim the only woman he's ever truly loved. With fire in his touch, he sets about convincing her to let him in once more, and this time he intends to keep her in his arms for always. An utterly delightful story from beginning to end, told with Linda's delicious sense of humor and sensitive touch.

In **RAISING HARRY,** LOVESWEPT #625 by Victoria Leigh, Griff Ross is a single father coping with the usual problems of raising a high-spirited three-year-old son. He's never been jealous of Harry until he finds him in the arms of their neighbor Sharron Capwell. Her lush mouth makes Griff long to kiss her breathless, while her soft curves tempt him with visions of bare shoulders touched only by moonlight and his hands. She makes him burn with pleasure as no woman ever has, but Griff, still hurt by a betrayal he's never forgiven, insists he wants only a friend and a lover. Single and childless, Sharron has always been content with her life—until she thrills to the ecstacy Griff shows her, and now finds herself struggling with her need to be his wife and Harry's mother. Rest assured that a happily-ever-after awaits these two, as well as the young one, once they admit the love they can't deny. Victoria tells a compelling love story, one you won't be able to put down.

Who can resist **THE COURTING COWBOY,** LOVESWEPT #626 by Glenna McReynolds? Ty Garrett is a rough-edged rancher who wants a woman to share the seasons, to love under the Colorado skies. But he expects that finding a lady in his middle-of-nowhere town would be very rough—until a spirited visiting teacher fascinates his son and captivates him too! Victoria Willoughby has beautiful skin, a very kissable mouth, and a sensual innocence that beckons Ty to woo her with fierce, possessive passion. He awakens her to pleasures she's never imagined, teaches her how wonderful taking chances can be, and makes her feel alluring, wanton. But she's already let one man rule her life and she's vowed never to belong to anyone ever again. Still, she knows that finding Ty is a miracle; now if she'll only realize that he's the best man and the right man for her . . . Glenna's talent shines brightly in this terrific romance.

Bonnie Pega begins her deliciously sexy novel, **THEN COMES MARRIAGE,** LOVESWEPT #627, with the hero and heroine meeting in a very unlikely place. Single mother-to-be Libby Austin certainly thinks that seeing the hunk of her dreams in a childbirth class is truly rotten luck, but she breathes a sigh of relief when she discovers that Zac Webster is coaching his sister-in-law, not his wife! His potent masculinity can charm every stitch of clothing off a woman's body; too bad he makes it all too clear that a child doesn't fit into his life. Still, unable to resist the temptation of Libby's blue velvet eyes and delectable smile, Zac lays siege to her senses, and her response of torrential kisses and fevered caresses drive him even wilder with hunger. Libby has given him more than he's hoped for—and a tricky dilemma. Can a man who's sworn off marriage and vows he's awful with kids claim a wildfire bride and her baby? With this wonderful romance, her second LOVESWEPT, Bonnie proves that she's a name to watch for.

There's no sexier **MAN AROUND THE HOUSE** than the hero in Cindy Gerard's upcoming LOVESWEPT, #628. Matthew Spencer is a lean, muscled heartbreaker, and when he answers his new next-door neighbor's cries for help, he finds himself rescuing disaster-prone Katie

McDonald, who's an accident waiting to happen—and a sassy temptress who's sure to keep him up nights. Awakening his hunger with the speed of a summer storm, Katie senses his pain and longs to comfort him, but Matthew makes her feel too much, makes her want more than she can have. Though she lets herself dare to dream of being loved, Katie knows she's all wrong for a man who's walking a careful path to regain custody of his son. He needs nice and normal, not her kind of wild and reckless—no matter that they sizzle in each other's arms. But Matthew's not about to give up a woman who adores his child, listens to his favorite golden oldie rock station, and gives him kisses that knock his socks off and make the stars spin. The magic of Cindy's writing shines through in this enchanting tale of love.

Finishing the line-up in a big way is Marcia Evanick and **IN DADDY'S ARMS,** LOVESWEPT #629. Brave enough to fight back from wounds inflicted in the line of duty, Bain O'Neill is devastated when doctors tell him he'll never be a father. Having a family is the only dream that ever mattered to him, a fantasy he can't give up, not when he knows that somewhere there are two children who are partly his, the result of an anonymous sperm donation he made years ago. A little investigation helps him locate his daughters—and their mother, Erin Flynn, a fiery-haired angel who tastes as good as she looks. Widowed for two years, Erin takes his breath away and heals him with her loving touch. Bain hates keeping the truth from her, and though the children soon beg him to be their daddy, he doesn't dare confess his secret to Erin, not until he's silenced her doubts about his love and makes her believe he's with her to stay forever. All the stirring emotions and funny touches that you've come to expect from Marcia are in this fabulous story.

On sale this month from Bantam are three spectacular women's novels. Dianne Edouard and Sandra Ware have teamed up once again and written **SACRED LIES,** a spellbinding novel of sin, seduction, and betrayal. Romany Chase is the perfect spy: intelligent, beautiful, a woman who thrills to the hunt. But with her latest mission, Romany is out of her depth. Adrift in a world where redemption may arrive too late, she is torn between the enigmatic priest she has orders to seduce and the fierce agent she desires. Beneath the glittering Roman moon, a deadly conspiracy of greed, corruption, and shattering evil is closing in, and Romany must choose whom to believe—and whom to love.

With more than several million copies of her novels in print, Kay Hooper is indisputably one of the best loved and popular authors of romantic fiction—and now she has penned **THE WIZARD OF SEATTLE,** a fabulous, magical story of immortal love and mesmerizing fantasy. Serena Smyth travels cross-country to Seattle to find Richard Patrick Merlin, guided by an instinct born of her determination to become a master wizard like him. She knows he can be her teacher, but she never expects the fire he ignites in her body and soul. Their love forbidden by an ancient law, Serena and Merlin will take a desperate gamble and travel to the long-lost world of Atlantis—to change the history that threatens to keep them apart for eternity.

From bestselling author Susan Johnson comes **SILVER FLAME,** the steamy sequel about the Braddock-Black dynasty you read about in **BLAZE.** Pick up a copy and find out why *Romantic Times* gave the author its Best Sensual Historical Romance Award. Sizzling with electrifying sensuality, **SILVER FLAME** burns hot! When Empress

Jordan is forced to sell her most precious possession to the highest bidder in order to feed her brothers and sisters, Trey Braddock-Black knows he must have her, no matter what the cost. The half-Absarokee rogue has no intention of settling down with one woman, but once he's spent three weeks with the sweet enchantress, he knows he can never give her up. . . .

Also on sale this month, in the hardcover edition from Doubleday, is **THE PAINTED LADY,** the stunningly sensual debut novel by Lucia Grahame. All of Paris and London recognize Fleur not only as Frederick Brooks's wife, but also as the successful painter's most inspiring model. But few know the secrets behind his untimely death and the terrible betrayal that leaves Fleur with a heart of ice—and no choice but to accept Sir Anthony Camwell's stunning offer: a fortune to live on in return for five nights of unrestrained surrender to what he plans to teach her—the exquisite art of love.

Happy reading!

With warmest wishes,

Nita Taublib

Nita Taublib
Associate Publisher
LOVESWEPT and FANFARE

Don't miss these exciting
books by your favorite
Bantam authors
On Sale in May:

SACRED LIES
by Dianne Edouard
and Sandra Ware

THE WIZARD OF SEATTLE
by Kay Hooper

SILVER FLAME
by Susan Johnson

"SPECIAL SNEAK PREVIEW"
THE MAGNIFICENT ROGUE
by Iris Johansen
On Sale in August

SACRED LIES
by Dianne Edouard and Sandra Ware

On Sale in May

Romany Chase is the perfect spy: intelligent, beautiful, a woman who thrills to the hunt. But torn between the fierce Israeli agent she desires and the enigmatic priest she has orders to seduce, Romany is out of her depth—adrift in a world where redemption may arrive too late . . . .

As soon as Romany opened the door, she knew she wasn't alone. Someone waited for her. Somewhere in the apartment.

She had never carried a gun. There had never been a need. Even though Sully could have gotten her easy clearance, and had more than once urged her to take along some insurance. But her assignments never warranted it. Except that one time, in Geneva, and that situation had come totally out of left field.

She allowed her eyes to become adjusted to the gloom and, easing herself against the wall, moved to the edge of the living room. She searched the shadows. Strained to see something behind the thick lumps and bumps of furniture. Nothing. She crouched lower and inched closer to the door opening into her bedroom.

She peered around the corner. Whoever was in the apartment had switched on the ceiling fan and the small lamp that sat on a dressing table in the adjoining bath. The soft light cast the room in semidarkness, and she could make out the large solid shape of a man. He reclined easily upon her bed, a marshmallowy heap of pillows propped against his back. He hadn't bothered to draw back the covers, and he lay on top of the spread completely naked.

She should have run, gotten out of her apartment as quickly as possible. Except she recognized the hard muscles under the deeply tanned skin, the black curling hair, the famous smirk that passed for a smile. Recognized the man who was a cold-blooded killer—and her lover.

Romany moved through the doorway and smiled. "I'm not even going to ask how you got in here, David."

She heard his dark laugh. "Is that any way to greet an old friend?"

She walked farther into the room and stood by the side of the bed. She stared into the bright green eyes, still a surprise after all this time. But then everything about David ben Haar was a surprise. "Why don't you make yourself comfortable?"

"I am . . . almost." He reached for her hand and ran it slowly down his chest, stopping just short of the black hair at his groin.

She glanced down, focusing on her hand, pale and thin clasped inside his. She could hear her breath catch inside her throat. And as if that sound had been meant as some sort of signal, he pulled her down beside him.

She rested with her back against him, letting him work the muscles at her shoulders, brush his lips against her hair. She didn't turn when she finally decided to speak. "What are you doing here, David?"

"I came to see you." The words didn't sound like a complete lie.

She twisted herself round to look up at him. "That's terribly flattering, David, but it won't work."

She watched the smirk almost stretch into a real smile.

"Okay, I came to make sure that Sully is taking good care of my girl."

"I'm not your girl, David." She tried not to sound mean, or hurt, or anything. But she could feel the muscles of his stomach tighten against her back.

"You know Sully's a fucking asshole," he said finally. "What's he waiting on, those jerks to open up a concentration camp and gas a few thousand Jews?"

"David, Sully's not an asshole. . . . Hey, what in the hell do you mean?" She jerked around, waiting for an answer, watching his eyes turn cold.

"Gimme a break, Romany."

"Dammit, David, I don't have the slightest idea what you're talking about. Besides, what in the hell have concentration camps got to do with . . . ?" She stopped short, not willing to play her hand, even though David probably knew all the cards she was holding.

"Well, Romany, I can save you, and Sully, and all your little friends over at the CIA a whole helluva lotta trouble. Somebody—and I think you're deaf, dumb, and blind if you haven't pegged who that is—is stealing the Church blind, swiping paintings right off the museum walls, then slipping by some pretty goddamn good fakes."

She watched him stare at her from inside the darkness of her bed, waiting with that flirting smirk on his mouth for her to say something. But she didn't answer.

" . . . And the SOB at the other end of this operation"—he was finishing what he'd started—"whether your CIA geniuses want to admit it or not, is black-marketing the genuine articles, funneling the profits to a group of neo-Nazis who aren't going to settle for German reunification."

"Neo-Nazis?"

She could hear him grit his teeth. "Yeah, neo-Nazis. Getting East and West Germany together was just the first stage of their nasty little operation. They've got big plans, Romany. But they're the same old fuckers. Just a little slicker."

"David, I can't believe—"

"Shit, you people never want to believe—"

"Stop it, David."

He dropped his head and took in a deep staccatoed breath. She felt his hands move up her arms to her shoulders and force her body close to his. "Sorry, Romany." He sounded hoarse. Then suddenly she felt him laughing against her. "You know something"—he was drawing back—"you're on the wrong side, Romany. We wouldn't have these stupid fights if you'd come and work with me. With the Mossad."

"Yeah? Work with you, huh? And just what inducement can you offer, David ben Haar?" She pulled away from him and stood up.

Her feelings about David were a tangled mess—which, after she'd watched him board the plane for Tel Aviv thirteen months ago, she'd thought she could safely leave unwound. But here he was again, still looking at her with that quizzical twist to his lips that she couldn't help but read as a challenge.

She wanted his hands on her. That was the thought that kept repeating itself, blotting out everything else in her mind. Her own hands trembled as she pushed the hair away from her neck and began to undo the buttons at her back. Undressing for him slowly, the way he liked it.

She hadn't let herself know how much she'd missed this, until she was beneath the covers naked beside him, and his hands were really on her again, taking control, his mouth moving everywhere on her body. The pulse of the ceiling fan blended suddenly with the rush of blood in her ears, and David's heat was under her skin like fire.

She pressed herself closer against him, her need for him blocking out her doubts. She wanted his solidness, his back under her hands, the hardness of him along the length of her body. David ben Haar, the perfect sexual fantasy. But real. Flesh and blood with eyes green as the sea. She looked into his eyes as he pulled her beneath him. There was no lightness in them now, only the same intensity of passion as when he killed. He came into her hard, and she shut her eyes, matching her rhythm to his. To dream was all right, as long as you didn't let it go beyond the borders of your bed.

* * *

With one small edge of the curtain rolled back, David ben Haar could just see through the balcony railing where the red Alfa Romeo Spider was waiting to park in the street. Romany had been flying about the apartment when the car had first driven up, still cursing him for her half-damp hair, amusingly anxious to keep the priest from getting as far as her door.

"I could hide in the bedroom." He had said it from his comfortable position, lying still naked on her sofa. Laughing at her as she went past buttoning her dress, hobbling on one shoe back to the bedroom.

"I don't trust you, David ben Haar." She'd come back with her other shoe and was throwing a hairbrush into that satchel she called a purse.

"Romany?" He had concentrated on the intent face, the wild curls threatening to break loose from the scarf that bound them. "Morrow one of the bad guys?"

Picking up a sweater, she had looked over at him then, with something remarkably like guilt. "I don't know." She was going for the door. "That's what I'm supposed to find out."

Then she was gone, her heels rat-tatting down the stairs. High heels at Villa d'Este. Just like an American. They never took anything seriously, then covered it up with a cynicism they hadn't earned. Romany was the flip side of that, of course, all earnestness and innocence. She was smart and she had guts. But it wouldn't be enough to protect her. He got up.

As he watched now, the Spider was swinging into the parking space that had finally become available at the curb. The door opened and a man got out, turning to where Romany had just emerged from under the balcony overhang. The man didn't exactly match the car, he looked far too American. What he didn't look like was a priest.

He watched them greet each other. Very friendly. The compressor on the air conditioner picked that minute to kick in again, so he couldn't hope to hear what was said. The man opened the passenger door for her, then walked around to get in. They didn't pull out right away, and he was wondering why when he saw the canvas top go down. The engine roared up as they shot away from the curb. He could tell by the tilt of her head that Romany was laughing.

They had not spoken for some time now, standing among the tall cypress, looking out below to the valley. The dying sun had painted everything in a kind of saturated light, and he seemed almost surreal standing next to her, his fair aureole of hair and tall body in light-colored shirt and slacks glowing against the blackness of the trees.

They had played today, she and Julian Morrow. Like happy strangers who had met in Rome, with no history and no future. She had felt it immediately, the playfulness, implicit in the red car, in the way he wore the light, casual clothes. Like an emblem, like a costume at a party.

She had sat in the red car, letting the wind blow everything away from her mind, letting it rip David from her body. Forgetting the job. Forgetting that the man beside her was a priest and a suspect, and she a paid agent of the United States government.

They had played today. And she had liked this uncomplicated persona better than any he had so far let her see. Liked his ease and his sense of humor, and the pleasure he had seemed to find in their joyful sharing of this place. She had to stop playing now, but this was the Julian Morrow she must hold in her mind. Not the priest. Not the suspect in criminal forgery. But a Julian Morrow to whom she could want to make love.

He turned to her and smiled. For a moment the truth of her treachery rose to stick in her throat. But she forced it down. This was her job. She was committed.

She smiled back, moving closer, as if she might want a better view, or perhaps some little shelter from the wind. He must have thought the latter, because she felt his hands draping her sweater more firmly around her shoulders.

Time to take the advantage. And shifting backward, she pressed herself lightly against his chest, her eyes closed. She was barely breathing, feeling for any answering strain. But she could find no sense of any rejection in his posture.

She turned. He was looking down at her. His eyes, so close, were unreadable. She would never remember exactly what had happened next, but she knew when her arms went around him. And the small moment of her triumph when she felt him hard against her. Then she was pulling him down toward her, her fingers tangling in his hair, her mouth moving on his.

At the moment when she ceased thinking at all, he let her go, suddenly, with a gesture almost brutal that set her tumbling back. His hand reached for her wrist, didn't let her fall. But the grip was not kind or gentle.

His face was closed. Completely. Anger would have been better. She was glad when he turned away from her, walking back in the direction of the car. There would be no dinner tonight at the wonderful terraced restaurant he had talked about today. Of that she was perfectly sure. It was going to be a long drive back to Rome.

THE WIZARD OF SEATTLE
the unique new romantic fantasy from
Kay Hooper

On Sale in May

In the bestselling tradition of the time-travel romances of Diana Gabaldon and Constance O'Day-Flannery, Kay Hooper creates her own fabulous, magical story of timeless love and mesmerizing fantasy.

She looked like a ragged, storm-drenched urchin, but from the moment Serena Smyth appeared on his Seattle doorstep Richard Patrick Merlin recognized the spark behind her green eyes, the wild talent barely held in check. And he would help her learn to control her gift, despite a taboo so ancient that the reasons for its existence had been forgotten. But he never suspected that in his rebellion he would risk all he had and all he was to feel a love none of his kind had ever known.

Seattle, 1984

It was his home. She knew that, although where her certainty came from was a mystery to her. Like the inner tug that had drawn her across the country to find him, the knowledge seemed instinctive, beyond words or reason. She didn't even know his name. But she knew what he was. He was what she wanted to be, needed to be, what all her instincts insisted she had to be, and only he could teach her what she needed to learn.

Until this moment, she had never doubted that he would accept her as his pupil. At sixteen, she was passing through that stage of development experienced by humans, twice in their lifetimes, a stage marked by total self-absorption and the unshakable certainty that the entire universe revolves around oneself. It occurred in infancy and in adolescence, but rarely ever again, unless one were utterly unconscious of reality. Those traits had given her the confidence she had needed in order to cross the country alone with no more than a ragged backpack and a few dollars.

But they deserted her now, as she stood at the wrought iron gates and stared up at the secluded old Victorian house. The rain beat down on her, and lightning flashed in the stormy sky, illuminating the turrets and gables of the house; there were few lighted windows, and those were dim rather than welcoming.

It *looked* like the home of a wizard.

She almost ran, abruptly conscious of her aloneness. But then she squared her thin shoulders, shoved open the gate, and walked steadily to the front door. Ignoring the bell, she used the brass knocker to rap sharply. The knocker was fashioned in the shape of an owl, the creature that symbolized wisdom, a familiar of wizards throughout fiction.

She didn't know about fact.

Her hand was shaking, and she gave it a fierce frown as she rapped the knocker once more against the solid door. She barely had time to release the knocker before the door was pulled open.

Tall and physically powerful, his raven hair a little shaggy and his black eyes burning with an inner fire, he surveyed the dripping, ragged girl on his doorstep with lofty disdain for long moments during which all of her determination melted away to nothing. Then he caught her collar with one elegant hand, much as he might have grasped a stray cat, and yanked her into the well-lit entrance hall. He studied her with daunting sternness.

What he saw was an almost painfully thin girl who looked much younger than her sixteen years. Her threadbare clothing was soaked; her short, tangled hair was so wet that only a hint of its normal vibrant red color was apparent; and her small face—all angles and seemingly filled with huge eyes—was white and pinched. She was no more attractive than a stray mongrel pup.

"Well?"

The vast poise of sixteen years deserted the girl as he barked the one word in her ear. She gulped. "I—I want to be a wizard," she managed finally, defiantly.

"Why?"

She was soaked to the skin, tired, hungry, and possessed a temper that had more than once gotten her into trouble. Her green eyes snapping, she glared up into his handsome, expressionless face, and her voice lost all its timidity.

"I *will* be a wizard! If you won't teach me, I'll find someone who will. I can summon fire already—a little—and I can *feel* the power inside me. All I need is a teacher, and I'll be great one day—"

He lifted her clear off the floor and shook her briefly, effortlessly, inducing silence with no magic at all. "The first lesson an apprentice must learn," he told her calmly, "is to never—ever—shout at a Master."

Then he casually released her, conjured a bundle of clothing out of thin air, and handed it to her. Then he waved a hand negligently and sent her floating up the dark stairs toward a bathroom.

And so it began.

Seattle, Present

His fingers touched her breasts, stroking soft skin and teasing the hard pink nipples. The swollen weight filled his hands as he lifted and kneaded, and when she moaned and arched her back, he lowered his mouth to her. He stopped thinking.

He felt. He felt his own body, taut and pulsing with desire, the blood hot in his veins. He felt her body, soft and warm and willing. He felt her hand on him, stroking slowly, her touch hungry and assured. Her moans and sighs filled his ears, and the heat of her need rose until her flesh burned. The tension inside him coiled more tightly, making his body ache, until he couldn't stand to wait another moment. He sank his flesh into hers, feeling her legs close strongly about his hips. Expertly, lustfully, she met his thrusts, undulating beneath him, her female body the cradle all men returned to. The heat between them built until it was a fever raging out of control, until his body was gripped by the inescapable, inexorable drive for release and pounded frantically inside her. Then, at last, the heat and tension drained from him in a rush . . .

Serena sat bolt upright in bed, gasping. In shock, she stared across the darkened room for a moment, and then she hurriedly leaned over and turned on the lamp on the nightstand. Blinking in the light, she held her hands up and stared at them, reassuring herself that they were hers, still slender and pale and tipped with neat oval nails.

They were hers. She was here and unchanged. Awake. Aware. Herself again.

She could still feel the alien sensations, still see the powerful bronzed hands against paler, softer skin, and still feel sensations her body was incapable of experiencing simply because she was female, not male—

And then she realized.

"Dear God . . . Richard," she whispered.

She had been inside his mind, somehow, in his head just like before, and he had been with another woman. He had been having sex with another woman. Serena had felt what he felt, from the sensual enjoyment of soft female flesh under his touch to the ultimate draining pleasure of orgasm. *She had felt what he felt.*

She drew her knees up and hugged them, feeling tears burn-ing her eyes and nausea churning in her stomach. Another woman. He had a woman somewhere, and she wasn't new because there had been a sense of familiarity in him, a certain knowledge. He knew this woman. Her skin was familiar, her taste, her desire. His body knew hers.

Even Master wizards, it seemed, had appetites just like other men.

Serena felt a wave of emotions so powerful she could endure them only in silent anguish. Her thoughts were tangled and fierce and raw. Not a monk, no, hardly a monk. In fact, it appeared he was quite a proficient lover, judging by the woman's response to him.

On her nightstand, the lamp's bulb burst with a violent sound, but she neither heard it nor noticed the return of darkness to the room.

So he was just a man after all, damn him, a man who got horny like other men and went to some woman who'd spread her legs for him. And often. His trips "out of town" were more frequent these last years. Oh, horny indeed . . .

Unnoticed by Serena, her television set flickered to life, madly scanned though all the channels, and then died with a sound as apologetic as a muffled cough.

Damn him. What'd he do, keep a mistress? Some pretty, pampered blonde—she had been blond, naturally—with emp-ty hot eyes who wore slinky nightgowns and crotchless panties, and moaned like a bitch in heat? Was there only one? Or had he bedded a succession of women over the years, keeping his reputation here in Seattle all nice and tidy while he satisfied his appetites elsewhere?

Serena heard a little sound, and was dimly shocked to realize it came from her throat. It sounded like that of an animal in pain, some tortured creature hunkered down in the dark as it waited helplessly to find out if it would live or die. She didn't realize that she was rocking gently. She didn't see her alarm clock flash a series of red numbers before going dark, or notice that her stereo system was spitting out tape from a cassette.

Only when the overhead light suddenly exploded was Serena jarred from her misery. With a tremendous effort, she struggled to control herself.

"Concentrate," she whispered. "Concentrate. Find the switch." And, for the first time, perhaps spurred on by her urgent need to control what she felt, she did find it. Her wayward energies stopped swirling all around her and were instantly drawn into some part of her she'd never recognized before, where they were completely and safely contained, held there in waiting without constant effort from her.

Moving stiffly, feeling exhausted, Serena got out of bed and moved cautiously across the room to her closet, trying to avoid the shards of glass sprinkled over the rugs and the polished wood floor. There were extra lightbulbs on the closet shelf, and she took one to replace the one from her nightstand lamp. It was difficult to unscrew the burst bulb, but she managed; she didn't trust herself to flick all the shattered pieces out of existence with her powers, not when she'd come so close to losing control entirely.

When the lamp was burning again, she got a broom and dustpan and cleaned up all the bits of glass. A slow survey of the room revealed what else she had destroyed, and she shivered a little at the evidence of just how dangerous unfocused power could be.

Ironically, she couldn't repair what she had wrecked, not by using the powers that had destroyed. Because she didn't understand the technology of television or radio or even clocks, it simply wasn't possible for her to focus her powers to fix what was broken. It would be like the blind trying to put together by touch alone something they couldn't even recognize enough to define.

To create or control anything, it was first necessary to understand its very elements, its basic structure, and how it functioned. How many times had Merlin told her that? Twenty times? A hundred?

Serena sat down on her bed, still feeling drained. But not numb; that mercy wasn't granted to her. The switch she had found to contain her energies could do nothing to erase the memory of Richard with another woman.

It hurt. She couldn't believe how much it hurt. All these years she had convinced herself that she was the only woman in his life who mattered, and now she knew that wasn't true. He didn't belong only to her. He didn't belong to her at all. He really didn't see her as a woman—or, if he did, she obviously held absolutely no attraction for him.

The pain was worse, knowing that.

Dawn had lightened the windows by the time Serena tried to go back to sleep. But she couldn't. She lay beneath the covers staring up at the ceiling, feeling older than she had ever felt before. There was no limbo now, no sense of being suspended between woman and child; Serena knew she could never again be a child, not even to protect herself.

The question was—how was that going to alter her relationship with Merlin? Could she pretend there was nothing different? No. Could she even bear to look at him without crying out her pain and rage? Probably not. How would he react when she made her feelings plain, with disgust or pity? That was certainly possible. Would her raw emotion drive him even farther away from her? Or was he, even now, planning to banish her from his life completely?

Because he knew. He knew what she had discovered in the dark watches of the night.

Just before her own shock had wrenched her free of his mind, Serena had felt for a split-second *his* shock as he sensed and recognized her presence intruding on that intensely private act.

He knew. He knew she had been there.

It was another part of her pain, the discomfiting guilt and

shame of having been, however unintentionally, a voyeur. She had a memory now that she would never forget, but it was his, not hers. She'd stolen it from him . . . . And of all the things they both had to face when he came home, that one was likely to be the most difficult of all.

The only certainty Serena could find in any of it was the knowledge that nothing would ever be the same again.

SILVER FLAME
by Susan Johnson

On Sale in May

She was driven by love to break every rule.... Empress
Jordan had fled to the Montana wilderness to escape a cruel
injustice, only to find herself forced to desperate means to
feed her brothers and sisters. Once she agreed to sell her most
precious possession to the highest bidder, she feared she'd made
a terrible mistake—even as she found herself hoping it was the
tall, dark, chiseled stranger who had taken her dare and claimed
her . . . .

Empress stood before him, unabashed in her nudity, and
raising her emerald eyes the required height to meet his so
far above, she said "What *will* you do with me, Mr. Braddock-
Black?"

"Trey," he ordered, unconscious of his lightly command-
ing tone.

"What *will* you do with me, Trey?" she repeated correcting
herself as ordered. But there was more than a hint of impudence in her tone and in her tilted mouth and arched brow.

Responding to the impudence with some of his own, he
replied with a small smile, "Whatever you prefer, Empress,
darling." He towered over her, clothed and booted, as dark
as Lucifer, and she was intensely aware of his power and size,
as if his presence seemed to invade her. "You set the pace,
sweetheart," he said encouragingly, reaching out to slide the

pad of one finger slowly across her shoulder. "But take your time," he went on, recognizing his own excitement, running his warm palm up her neck and cupping the back of her head lightly. Trey's voice had dropped half an octave. "We've three weeks. . . ." And for the first time in his life he looked forward to three undiluted weeks of one woman's company. It was like scenting one's mate, primordial and reflexive, and while his intellect ignored the peremptory, inexplicable compulsion, his body and blood and dragooned sensory receptors willingly complied to the urgency.

Bending his head low, his lips touched hers lightly, brushing twice across them like silken warmth before he gently slid over her mouth with his tongue and sent a shocking trail of fire curling deep down inside her.

She drew back in an unconscious response, but he'd felt the heated flame, too, and from the startled look in his eyes she knew the spark had touched them both. Trey's breathing quickened, his hand tightened abruptly on the back of her head, pulling her closer with insistence, with authority, while his other hand slid down her back until it rested warmly at the base of her spine. And when his mouth covered hers a second time, intense suddenly, more demanding, she could feel him rising hard against her. She may have been an innocent in the ways of a man and a woman, but Empress knew how animals mated in nature, and for the first time she sensed a soft warmth stirring within herself.

It was at once strange and blissful, and for a brief detached moment she felt very grown, as if a riddle of the universe were suddenly revealed. One doesn't have to love a man to feel the fire, she thought. It was at odds with all her mother had told her. Inexplicably she experienced an overwhelming sense of discovery, as if she alone knew a fundamental principle of humanity. But then her transient musing was abruptly arrested, for under the light pressure of Trey's lips she found hers opening, and the velvety, heated caress of Trey's tongue slowly entered her mouth, exploring languidly, licking her sweetness, and the heady, brandy taste of him was like a fresh treasure to be savored. She tentatively responded like a lambkin to new, unsteady legs, and when her tongue brushed his and did her own unhurried tasting, she heard him groan low in his throat. Swaying gently against her, his hard length pressed more adamantly into her yielding softness. Fire raced downward to a tingling place deep inside her as Trey's strong, insistent arousal throbbed against the soft curve of her stomach. He held her captive with his large hand low on her back as they kissed, and she felt a leaping flame speed along untried nerve endings, creating delicious new sensations. There was strange pleasure in the feel of his soft wool shirt; a melting warmth seeped through her senses, and she swayed closer into the strong male body, as if she knew instinctively that he would rarefy the enchantment. A moment later, as her mouth opened pliantly beneath his, her hands came up of their own accord and, rich with promise, rested lightly on his shoulders.

Her artless naïveté was setting his blood dangerously afire. He gave her high marks for subtlety. First the tentative withdrawal, and now the ingenuous response, was more erotic than any flagrant vice of the most skilled lover. And yet it surely must be some kind of drama, effective like the scene downstairs, where she withheld more than she offered in the concealing men's clothes and made every man in the room want to undress her.

Whether artifice, pretext, sham, or entreating supplication, the soft, imploring body melting into his, the small appealing hands warm on his shoulders, made delay suddenly inconvenient. "I think, sweet Empress," he said, his breath warm on her mouth, "*next* time you can set the pace. . . ."

Bending quickly, he lifted her into his arms and carried her to the bed. Laying her down on the rose velvet coverlet, he stood briefly and looked at her. Wanton as a Circe nymph, she looked back at him, her glance direct into his heated gaze, and she saw the smoldering, iridescent desire in his eyes. She was golden pearl juxtaposed to blush velvet, and when she slowly lifted her arms to him, he, no longer in control of himself, not detached or casual or playful as he usually was making love, took a deep breath, swiftly moved the half step to the bed, and lowered his body over hers, reaching for the buttons on his trousers with trembling fingers. His boots crushed the fine velvet but he didn't notice; she whimpered slightly when his heavy gold belt buckle pressed into her silken skin, but he kissed her in apology, intent on burying himself in the devastating Miss Jordan's lushly carnal body. His wool-clad legs pushed her pale thighs apart, and all he could think of was the feel of her closing around him. He surged forward, and she cried out softly. Maddened with desire, he thrust forward again. This time he *heard* her cry. "Oh, Christ," he breathed, urgent need suffocating in his lungs, "you can't be a virgin." He never bothered with virgins. It had been years since he'd slept with one. Lord, he was hard.

"It doesn't matter," she replied quickly, tense beneath him.

"It doesn't matter," he repeated softly, blood drumming in his temples and in his fingertips and in the soles of his feet inside the custom-made boots, and most of all in his rigid erection, insistent like a battering ram a hair's breadth from where he wanted to be so badly, he could taste the blood in his mouth. It doesn't matter, his conscience repeated. She said it doesn't matter, so it doesn't matter, and he drove in again.

Her muffled cry exploded across his lips as his mouth lowered to kiss her.

"Oh, hell." He exhaled deeply, drawing back, and, poised on his elbows, looked down at her uncertainly, his long dark hair framing his face like black silk.

"I won't cry out again," she whispered, her voice more certain than the poignant depths of her shadowy eyes. "Please . . . I must have the money."

It was all too odd and too sudden and too out of charac-ter for him. Damn . . . plundering a virgin, making her cry in fear and pain. *Steady, you'll live if you don't have her*, he told himself, but quivering need played devil's advocate to that platitude. She was urging him on. His body was even more fiercely demanding he take her. "Hell and damnation," he muttered disgruntedly. The problem was terrible, demand-ing immediate answers, and he wasn't thinking too clearly, only feeling a delirious excitement quite detached from moral judgment. And adamant. "Bloody hell," he breathed, and in that moment, rational thought gained a fingertip control on the ragged edges of his lust. "Keep the money. I don't want to—" He said it quickly, before he'd change his mind, then paused and smiled. "Obviously that's not entirely true, but I don't ruin virgins," he said levelly.

Empress had not survived the death of her parents and the months following, struggling to stay alive in the wilderness, without discovering in herself immense strength. She sum-moned it now, shakily but determinedly. "It's not a mor-al dilemma. It's a business matter and my responsibility. I insist."

He laughed, his smile close and deliciously warm. "Here I'm refusing a woman insisting I take her virginity. I must be crazy."

"The world's crazy sometimes, I think," she replied softly, aware of the complex reasons prompting her conduct.

"Tonight, at least," he murmured, "it's more off track than usual." But even for a wild young man notorious as a womaniz-er, the offered innocence was too strangely bizarre. And maybe too businesslike for a man who found pleasure and delight in the act. It was not flattering to be a surrogate for a business matter. "Look," he said with an obvious effort, "thanks but no thanks. I'm not interested. But keep the money. I admire your courage." And rolling off her, he lay on his back and shouted, "*Flo!*"

"No!" Empress cried, and was on top of him before he drew his next breath, terrified he'd change his mind about the money, terrified he'd change his mind in the morning when his head was clear and he woke up in Flo's arms. Fifty thousand dollars was a huge sum of money to give away on a whim, or to lose to some misplaced moral scruple. She must convince him to stay with her, then at least she could earn the money. Or at least try.

Lying like silken enchantment on his lean, muscled body, she covered his face with kisses. Breathless, rushing kisses, a young girls's simple closemouthed kisses. Then, in a flush of boldness, driven by necessity, a tentative dancing lick of her small tongue slid down his straight nose, to his waiting mouth. When her tongue lightly caressed the arched curve of his upper lip, his hands came up and closed on her naked shoulders, and he drew the teasing tip into his mouth. He sucked on it gently, slowly, as if he envisioned a lifetime without interruptions, until the small, sun-kissed shoulders beneath his hands trembled in tiny quivers.

Strange, fluttering wing beats sped through her heating blood, and a curious languor caused Empress to twine her arms around Trey's strong neck. But her heart was beating hard like the Indian drums whose sound carried far up to their hidden valley in summer, for fear outweighed languor still. He mustn't go to Flo. Slipping her fingers through the black luster of his long hair, ruffled in loose waves on his neck, she brushed her mouth along his cheek. "Please," she whispered near his ear, visions of her hope to save her family dashed by his reluctance, "stay with me." It was a simple plea, simply put. It was perhaps her last chance. Her lips traced the perfect curve of his ears, and his hands tightened their grip in response. "Say it's all right. Say I can stay. . . ." She was murmuring rapidly in a flurry of words.

How should he answer the half-shy, quicksilver words? Why was she insisting? Why did the flattery of a woman wanting him matter?

Then she shifted a little so her leg slid between his, a sensual, instinctive movement, and the smooth velvet of his masculinity rose against her thigh. It was warm, it was hot, and like a child might explore a new sensation, she moved her leg lazily up its length.

Trey's mouth went dry, and he couldn't convince himself that refusal was important any longer. He groaned, thinking, there are some things in life without answers. His hand was trembling when he drew her mouth back to his.

A moment later, when Flo knocked and called out his name, Empress shouted, "Go away!" And when Flo repeated his name, Trey's voice carried clearly through the closed door. "I'll be down later."

He was rigid but tense and undecided, and Empress counted on the little she knew about masculine desire to accomplish what her logical explanation hadn't. Being French, she was well aware that *amour* could be heated and fraught with urgent emotion, but she was unsure exactly about the degree of urgency relative to desire.

But she knew what had happened moments before when she'd tasted his mouth and recalled how he'd responded to her yielding softness, so she practiced her limited expertise with a determined persistence. She must be sure she had the money. And if it would assure her family their future, her virginity was paltry stuff in the bargain.

"Now let's begin again," she whispered.

THE MAGNIFICENT ROGUE
by Iris Johansen

On Sale in August

From the glittering court of Queen Elizabeth to the barren island of Craighdu, THE MAGNIFICENT ROGUE is the spellbinding story of courageous love and unspeakable evil. The daring chieftain of a Scottish clan, Robert MacDarren knows no fear, and only the threat to a kinsman's life makes him bow to Queen Elizabeth's order that he wed Kathryn Ann Kentrye. He's aware of the dangerous secret in Kate's past, a secret that could destroy a great empire, but he doesn't expect the stirring of desire when he first lays eyes on the fragile beauty. Grateful to escape the tyranny of her guardian, Kate accepts the mesmerizing stranger as her husband. But even as they discover a passion greater than either has known, enemies are weaving their poisonous web around them, and soon Robert and Kate must risk their very lives to defy the ultimate treachery.

In the following scene, Robert and his cousin Gavin Gordon have come to Kate's home to claim her—and she flees.

She was being followed!

Sebastian?

Kate paused a moment on the trail and caught a glimpse of dark hair and the shimmer of the gold necklace about her pursuer's neck. Not Sebastian. Robert MacDarren.

The wild surge of disappointment she felt at the realization was completely unreasonable. He must have come at Sebastian's bidding, which meant her guardian had persuaded him to his way of thinking. Well, what had she expected? He was a stranger and Sebastian was a respected man of the cloth. There was no reason why he would be different from any of the others. How clever of Sebastian to send someone younger and stronger than himself to search her out, she thought bitterly.

She turned and began to run, her shoes sinking into the mud with every step. She glanced over her shoulder.

He was closer. He was not running, but his long legs covered the ground steadily, effortlessly, as his gaze studied the trail in front of him. He had evidently not seen her yet and was only following her tracks.

She was growing weaker. Her head felt peculiarly light and her breath was coming in painful gasps. She couldn't keep running.

And she couldn't surrender.

Which left only one solution to her dilemma. She sprinted several yards ahead and then darted into the underbrush at the side of the trail.

Hurry. She had to hurry. Her gaze frantically searched the underbrush. Ah, there was one.

She pounced on a heavy branch and then backtracked several yards and held it, waiting.

She must aim for the head. She had the strength for only one blow and it must drop him.

Her breath sounded heavily and terribly loud. She had to breathe more evenly or he would hear her.

He was almost upon her.

Her hands tightened on the branch.

He went past her, his expression intent as he studied the tracks.

She drew a deep breath, stepped out on the trail behind him, and swung the branch with all her strength.

He grunted in pain and then slowly crumpled to the ground.

She dropped the branch and ran past his body and darted down the trail again.

Something struck the back of her knees. She was falling!

She hit the ground so hard, the breath left her body. Blackness swirled around her.

When the darkness cleared, she realized she was on her back, her arms pinned on each side of her head. Robert MacDarren was astride her body.

She started to struggle.

"Lie still, dammit." His hands tightened cruelly on her arms. "I'm not—Ouch!"

She had turned her head and sunk her teeth into his wrist. She could taste the coppery flavor of blood in her mouth, but his grip didn't ease.

"Let me go!" How stupidly futile the words were when she knew he had no intention of releasing her.

She tried to butt her head against his chest, but she couldn't reach him.

"Really, Robert, can't you wait until the words are said for you to climb on top of her?" Gavin Gordon said from behind MacDarren.

"It's about time you got here," MacDarren said in a growl. "She's trying to kill me."

'Aye, for someone who couldn't lift her head, she's doing quite well. I saw her strike the blow." Gavin grinned. "But I was too far away to come to your rescue. Did she do any damage?"

"I'm going to have one hell of a headache."

Kate tried to knee him in the groin, but he quickly moved upward on her body.

"Your hand's bleeding," Gavin observed.

"She's taken a piece out of me. I can see why Landfield kept the ropes on her."

The ropes. Despair tore through her as she realized how completely Sebastian had won him to his way of thinking. The man would bind her and take her back to Sebastian. She couldn't fight against both MacDarren and Gordon and would use the last of her precious strength trying to do so. She would have to wait for a better opportunity to present itself. She stopped fighting and lay there staring defiantly at him.

"Very sensible," MacDarren said grimly. "I'm not in a very good temper at the moment. I don't think you want to make it worse."

"Get off me."

"And have you run away again?" MacDarren shook his head. "You've caused me enough trouble for one day. Give me your belt, Gavin."

Gavin took off his wide leather belt and handed it to MacDarren, who buckled the belt about her wrists and drew it tight.

"I'm not going back to the cottage," she said with the fierceness born of desperation. "I *can't* go back there."

He got off her and rose to his feet. "You'll go where I tell you to go, even if I have to drag—" He stopped in self-disgust as he realized what he had said. "Christ, I sound like that bastard." The anger suddenly left him as he looked at her lying there before him. "You're afraid of him?"

Fear was always with her when she thought of Sebastian, but she would not admit it. She sat up and repeated, "I can't go back."

He studied her for a moment. "All right, we won't go back. You'll never have to see him again."

She stared at him in disbelief.

He turned to Gavin. "We'll stay the night at that inn we passed at the edge of the village. Go back to the cottage and get her belongings and then saddle the horses. We'll meet you at the stable."

Gavin nodded and the next moment disappeared into the underbrush.

MacDarren glanced down at Kate. "I trust you don't object to that arrangement?"

She couldn't comprehend his words. "You're taking me away?"

"If you'd waited, instead of jumping out the window, I would have told you that two hours ago. That's why I came."

Then she thought she understood. "You're taking me to the lady?"

He shook his head. "It appears Her Majesty thinks it's time you wed."

Shock upon shock. "Wed?"

He said impatiently, "You say that as if you don't know what it means. You must have had instructions on the duties of wifehood."

"I know what it means." Slavery and suffocation and cruelty. From what she could judge from Sebastian and Martha's marriage, a wife's lot was little better than her own. True, he did not beat Martha, but the screams she heard from their bedroom while they mated had filled her with sick horror. But she had thought she would never have to worry about that kind of mistreatment. "I can never marry."

"Is that what the good vicar told you?" His lips tightened. "Well, it appears the queen disagrees."

Then it might come to pass. Even Sebastian obeyed the queen. The faintest hope began to spring within her. Even though marriage was only another form of slavery, perhaps the queen had chosen an easier master than Sebastian for her. "Who am I to marry?"

He smiled sardonically. "I have that honor."

Another shock and not a pleasant one. Easy was not a term anyone would use to describe this man. She blurted, "And you're not afraid?"

"Afraid of you? Not if I have someone to guard my back."

That wasn't what she meant, but of course he wouldn't be afraid. She doubted if he feared anything or anyone, and, besides, she wasn't what Sebastian said she was. He had said the words so often, she sometimes found herself believing him, and she was so tired now, she wasn't thinking clearly. The strength was seeping out of her with every passing second. "No, you shouldn't be afraid." She swayed. "Not Lilith . . ."

"More like a muddy gopher," he muttered as he reached out and steadied her. "We have to get to the stable. Can you walk, or shall I carry you?"

"I can walk." She dismissed the outlandish thought of marriage from her mind. She would ponder the implications of this change in her life later. There were more important matters to consider now. "But we have to get Caird."

"Caird? Who the devil is Caird?"

"My horse." She turned and started through the underbrush. "Before we go I have to fetch him. He's not far. . . ."

She could hear the brush shift and whisper as he followed her. "Your horse is in the forest?"

"I was hiding him from Sebastian. He was going to kill him. He wanted me to tell him where he was."

"And that was why he was dragging you?"

She ignored the question. "Sebastian said the forest beasts would devour him. He frightened me." She was staggering with exhaustion, but she couldn't give up now. "It's been such a while since I left him." She rounded a corner of a trail and breathed a sigh of relief as she caught sight of Caird calmly munching grass under the shelter of an oak tree. "No, he's fine."

"You think so?" MacDarren's skeptical gaze raked the piebald stallion from its swayback to its knobby knees. "I see nothing fine about him. How old is he?"

"Almost twenty." She reached the horse and tenderly began to stroke his muzzle. "But he's strong and very good-tempered."

"He won't do," MacDarren said flatly. "We'll have to get rid of him. He'd never get through the Highlands. We'll leave him with the innkeeper and I'll buy you another horse."

"I *won't* get rid of him," she said fiercely. "I can't just leave him. How would I know if they'd take good care of him? He goes with us."

"And I say he stays."

The words were spoken with such absolute resolution that they sent a jolt of terror through her. They reminded her of Sebastian's edicts, from which there was no appeal. She moistened her lips. "Then I'll have to stay too."

MacDarren's gaze narrowed on her face. "And what if Landfield catches you again?"

She shrugged and leaned her cheek wearily against Caird's muzzle. "He belongs to me," she said simply.

She could feel his gaze on her back and sensed his exasperation. "Oh, for God's sake!" He picked up her saddle from the ground by the tree and threw it on Caird's back. He began to buckle the cinches. "All right, we'll take him."

Joy soared through her. "Truly?"

"I said it, didn't I?" He picked her up and tossed her into the saddle. "We'll use him as a pack horse and I'll get you another mount to ride. Satisfied?"

Satisfied! She smiled brilliantly. "Oh yes. You won't regret it. But you needn't spend your money on another horse. Caird is really very strong. I'm sure he'll be able to—"

"I'm already regretting it." His tone was distinctly edgy as he began to lead the horse through the forest. "Even carrying a light load, I doubt if he'll get through the Highlands."

It was the second time he had mentioned these forbidding Highlands, but she didn't care where they were going as long as they were taking Caird. "But you'll do it? You won't change your mind?"

For an instant his expression softened as he saw the eagerness in her face. "I won't change my mind."

Gavin was already mounted and waiting when they arrived at the stable a short time later. A grin lit his face as he glanced from Kate to the horse and then back again. "Hers?"

Robert nodded. "And the cause of all this turmoil."

"A fitting pair," Gavin murmured. "She has a chance of cleaning up decently, but the horse . . ." He shook his head. "No hope for it, Robert."

"My thought exactly. But we're keeping him anyway."

Gavin's brows lifted. "Oh, are we? Interesting . . ."

Robert swung into the saddle. "Any trouble with the vicar and his wife?"

Kate's hands tensed on the reins.

"Mistress Landfield appeared to be overjoyed to give me the girl's belongings." He nodded at a small bundle tied to the saddle. "And the vicar just glowered at me."

"Perhaps he's given up."

"He won't give up," Kate whispered. "He never gives up."

"Then perhaps we'd better go before we encounter him again," Robert said as he kicked his horse into a trot. "Keep an eye on her, Gavin. She's almost reeling in that saddle."

Sebastian was waiting for them a short distance from the cottage. He stood blocking the middle of the path.

"Get out of the way," Robert said coldly. "I'm not in the mood for this."

"It's your last chance," Sebastian said. "Give her back to me before it's too late."

"Stand aside, Landfield."

"Kathryn." Sebastian turned to her and his voice was pleading. "Do not go. You know you can never wed. You know what will happen."

Robert rode forward and his horse's shoulder forced Sebastian to the side of the trail. He motioned Gavin and Kate to ride ahead. "It's over. She's no longer your responsibility." His voice lowered to soft deadliness. "And if you ever approach her again, I'll make sure I never see you repeat the mistake."

"You'll see me." Landfield's eyes shimmered with tears as his gaze clung to Kate. "I wanted to spare you, Kathryn. I wanted to save you, but God has willed otherwise. You know what has to be done now."

He turned and walked heavily back toward the cottage.

"What did he mean?" Gavin asked as his curious gaze followed Landfield.

She didn't answer as she watched Sebastian stalk away. She realized she was shivering with a sense of impending doom. How foolish. This was what he wanted her to feel, his way of chaining her to him.

"Well?" Robert asked.

"Nothing. He just wanted to make me afraid." She moistened her lips. "He likes me to be afraid of him."

She could see he didn't believe her and thought he would pursue it. Instead he said quietly, "You don't have to fear him any longer. He no longer holds any power over you." He held her gaze with a mesmerizing power. "I'm the only one who does now."

OFFICIAL RULES TO WINNERS CLASSIC SWEEPSTAKES

No Purchase necessary. To enter the sweepstakes follow instructions found elsewhere in this offer. You can also enter the sweepstakes by hand printing your name, address, city, state and zip code on a 3" x 5" piece of paper and mailing it to: Winners Classic Sweepstakes, P.O. Box 785, Gibbstown, NJ 08027. Mail each entry separately. Sweepstakes begins 12/1/91. Entries must be received by 6/1/93. Some presentations of this sweepstakes may feature a deadline for the Early Bird prize. If the offer you receive does, then to be eligible for the Early Bird prize your entry must be received according to the Early Bird date specified. Not responsible for lost, late, damaged, misdirected, illegible or postage due mail. Mechanically reproduced entries are not eligible. All entries become property of the sponsor and will not be returned.

Prize Selection/Validations: Winners will be selected in random drawings on or about 7/30/93, by VENTURA ASSOCIATES, INC., an independent judging organization whose decisions are final. Odds of winning are determined by total number of entries received. Circulation of this sweepstakes is estimated not to exceed 200 million. Entrants need not be present to win. All prizes are guaranteed to be awarded and delivered to winners. Winners will be notified by mail and may be required to complete an affidavit of eligibility and release of liability which must be returned within 14 days of date of notification or alternate winners will be selected. Any guest of a trip winner will also be required to execute a release of liability. Any prize notification letter or any prize returned to a participating sponsor, Bantam Doubleday Dell Publishing Group, Inc., its participating divisions or subsidiaries, or VENTURA ASSOCIATES, INC. as undeliverable will be awarded to an alternate winner. Prizes are not transferable. No multiple prize winners except as may be necessary due to unavailability, in which case a prize of equal or greater value will be awarded. Prizes will be awarded approximately 90 days after the drawing. All taxes, automobile license and registration fees, if applicable, are the sole responsibility of the winners. Entry constitutes permission (except where prohibited) to use winners' names and likenesses for publicity purposes without further or other compensation.

Participation: This sweepstakes is open to residents of the United States and Canada, except for the province of Quebec. This sweepstakes is sponsored by Bantam Doubleday Dell Publishing Group, Inc. (BDD), 666 Fifth Avenue, New York, NY 10103. Versions of this sweepstakes with different graphics will be offered in conjunction with various solicitations or promotions by different subsidiaries and divisions of BDD. Employees and their families of BDD, its division, subsidiaries, advertising agencies, and VENTURA ASSOCIATES, INC., are not eligible.

Canadian residents, in order to win, must first correctly answer a time limited arithmetical skill testing question. Void in Quebec and wherever prohibited or restricted by law. Subject to all federal, state, local and provincial laws and regulations.

Prizes: The following values for prizes are determined by the manufacturers' suggested retail prices or by what these items are currently known to be selling for at the time this offer was published. Approximate retail values include handling and delivery of prizes. Estimated maximum retail value of prizes: 1 Grand Prize ($27,500 if merchandise or $25,000 Cash); 1 First Prize ($3,000); 5 Second Prizes ($400 each); 35 Third Prizes ($100 each); 1,000 Fourth Prizes ($9.00 each); 1 Early Bird Prize ($5,000); Total approximate maximum retail value is $50,000. Winners will have the option of selecting any prize offered at level won. Automobile winner must have a valid driver's license at the time the car is awarded. Trips are subject to space and departure availability. Certain black-out dates may apply. Travel must be completed within one year from the time the prize is awarded. Minors must be accompanied by an adult. Prizes won by minors will be awarded in the name of parent or legal guardian.

For a list of Major Prize Winners (available after 7/30/93): send a self-addressed, stamped envelope entirely separate from your entry to: Winners Classic Sweepstakes Winners, P.O. Box 825, Gibbstown, NJ 08027. Requests must be received by 6/1/93. DO NOT SEND ANY OTHER CORRESPONDENCE TO THIS P.O. BOX.

Don't miss these fabulous Bantam women's fiction titles on sale in June

LADY VALIANT

☐ 29575-6 $5.50/6.50 in Canada

by Suzanne Robinson

Bestselling author of LADY DEFIANT

"An author with star quality....Spectacularly talented."
—*Romantic Times*

*Once Mary, Queen of Scots, had been her closest friend.
Now Thea Hunt was determined to pay back the queen's
kindness—by journeying to Scotland to warn her away from
a treacherous marriage. But in the thick of an English forest,
Thea suddenly finds herself set upon by thieves...and
chased down by a golden-haired highwayman who'd still her
struggles—and stir her heart—with one penetrating glance
from his fiery blue eyes.*

MASK OF NIGHT

☐ 29062-2 $4.99/5.99/6.50 in Canada

by Lois Wolfe

Author of THE SCHEMERS

*"Fast paced, highly evocative, filled with action, surprises,
and shocking revelations....an intriguing, different Civil War
romance."*   —*Romantic Times* on *The Schemers*

*In St. Louis in the late 1800s, a fair-haired beauty and a
bankrupt cattleman hell-bent on revenge are drawn to each
other across the footlights...but the heat of their passion
would ignite a fire that could burn them both.*

Ask for these books at your local bookstore or use this page to order.

The Very Best In Contemporary Women's Fiction

Sandra Brown

_____	29085-1 22 INDIGO PLACE	$4.50/5.50 in Canada
_____	56045-X TEMPERATURES RISING	$5.99/6.99
_____	28990-X TEXAS! CHASE	$5.99/6.99
_____	28951-9 TEXAS! LUCKY	$5.99/6.99
_____	29500-4 TEXAS! SAGE	$5.99/6.99
_____	29783-X A WHOLE NEW LIGHT	$5.99/6.99

Tami Hoag

_____	29534-9 LUCKY'S LADY	$4.99/ 5.99
_____	29053-3 MAGIC	$4.99/ 5.99
_____	29272-2 STILL WATERS	$4.99/ 5.99
_____	56050-6 SARAH'S SIN	$4.50/ 5.50

Nora Roberts

_____	27283-7 BRAZEN VIRTUE	$4.99/5.99
_____	29597-7 CARNAL INNOCENCE	$5.50/6.50
_____	29490-3 DIVINE EVIL	$5.99/6.99
_____	29078-9 GENUINE LIES	$4.99/5.99
_____	26461-3 HOT ICE	$4.99/5.99
_____	28578-5 PUBLIC SECRETS	$4.95/5.95
_____	26574-1 SACRED SINS	$5.50/6.50
_____	27859-2 SWEET REVENGE	$5.50/6.50

Pamela Simpson

_____	29424-5 FORTUNE'S CHILD	$5.99/6.99

Deborah Smith

_____	29690-6 BLUE WILLOW	$5.50/ 6.50
_____	29092-4 FOLLOW THE SUN	$4.99/ 5.99
_____	29107-6 MIRACLE	$4.50/ 5.50

Ask for these titles at your bookstore or use this page to order.

Please send me the books I have checked above. I am enclosing $ _____ (add $2.50 to cover postage and handling). Send check or money order, no cash or C. O. D.'s please.

Mr./ Ms. _____

Address _____

City/ State/ Zip _____

Send order to: Bantam Books, Dept. FN24, 2451 S. Wolf Road, Des Plaines, IL 60018

Please allow four to six weeks for delivery.

Prices and availability subject to change without notice.

FN 24 - 3/93